Evelyn Kaltenbach

Hotel Silvretta

A Novel

For my children Melanie, Patrick and Pascal

And in memory of Giorgio Rocco

Other books by Evelyn Kaltenbach

Beyond the Blue	2000	Novel
Between the Moon	2009	Poems
Meanderings of the Soul	2010	Poems & Photography
Wings of Friendship	2013	Poems & Photography
Never Trust a Sagittarius	2014	Short Story
Broken Open	2018	Poems & Photography
Limlight	2020	Poems & Photography
Das Zimmer zum Park	2022	Novel (German Edition)
Ode to Life	2023	Poems & Photography

Hotel Silvretta

A Novel

When we step back

from our ordinary view

the world reveals

the big picture

We begin to see

with eyes wide open

how magnificent

how fragile

how mysterious

our lives are

And we finally

catch a glimpse

of the grandeur

of the universe

— Maja Rim, Collected Poems

Overture

February 2022

Klosters celebrated its 800-year anniversary. Natalie didn't want anything to do with it. She felt comfortable in her beautiful, bright apartment on Grellingerstrasse in Basel. She had her small, close circle of friends and fulfilling volunteer work in animal welfare. Nevertheless. Natalie turned 70 that year, and she had not visited Klosters in almost 50 years.

Klosters. Natalie loved the pretty village in the upper Prättigau with her heart and soul. She had spent the best years of her youth there, in all seasons. She remembered exactly the order of the villages driving up the Prättigau by car or by the Rhaetian Railway: Seewis, Grüsch, Schiers, Jenaz, Fideris, Küblis, Saas, Serneus, Klosters-Dorf and finally Klosters-Platz. Every time Natalie arrived it felt as if she could finally breathe again. That well known tingling bliss bubbled up from her core and suffused every pore of her being. She was home.

Klosters. Natalie's Papi used to proudly tell everyone who cared to listen that Klosters had acquired the name "Hollywood on the Rocks" in the 1950s. At that time, the crème de la crème of film stars, writers and royalty met and mingled in the village and on the slopes: Gene Kelly, Audrey Hepburn, Julie Andrews, Rex Harrison, Peter Sellers, David Niven, Paul Newman, Deborah Kerr, Irwin Shaw, Lex Barker, Greta Garbo, Yul Brynner, Françoise Sagan; and much later Prince Charles and Lady Di.

Papi knew that Gene Kelly had danced on the tables at the Chesa Grischuna. That Deborah Kerr had been married to Peter Viertel in Klosters. That Irwin Shaw had written many of his novels in Klosters, also at the Hotel Silvretta. That Roger Vadim had landed in Klosters by helicopter. That Ruth Guler had ruled the celebrity with an iron fist in the famous Wynegg and served them with her mountain charm. And that Prince Charles was a fantastic skier.

Klosters. According to the 800th Anniversary website, the Church of St. Jakob was first mentioned in a document in 1222, and was expanded into a monastery by members of the Premonstratensian Order. Thus, 1222 is considered the year of foundation of Klosters. In the same century, the first Walser settlers appeared in the area of the monastery of St. Jakob. Natalie loved the sunburned wooden Walser houses in Klosters, Selfranga and Monbiel, which were still inhabited today and whose windows were decorated with an abundance of red, white and pink geraniums in summer.

Klosters. Already in the 70s of the 19th century Klosters was mentioned several times as a health resort. Josias Mattli, the founder of the Kuranstalt J. Mattli – Hotel Silvretta and Kurhaus, was one of the greatest initiators of Klosters as a summer vacation destination. On 9 October 1889, the Landquart-Klosters section of the Rhaetian Railway (then called the Landquart-Davos Railway) was opened, and Klosters became accessible in a fast and pleasant way. Both the Hotel Silvretta and the Hotel Vereina opened their doors to winter guests in the early 20th century.

The old Hotel Silvretta in Klosters was Natalie's refuge.

It had charm and tradition. She knew the reception, the dining room, the bar, the main building and the Kurhaus, the Hübel and the Sunny Corner, the games room and the magnificent park with the tennis courts better than her home in Basel. She had also met Roman at the Silvretta. Roman Camenisch, waiter. And so much more.

* * *

On this cool February morning in 2022, Natalie called the (new) Hotel Silvretta in Klosters. She heard a friendly voice at the other end of the wire:

"Silvretta Parkhotel Klosters, good morning. My name is Anja, how may I help you?"

"Good morning. My name is Natalie Steiner. I would like to book room 408 for two weeks in February. When would it be available?"

"Mrs. Steiner, actually, room 408 would be fully booked until the end of March. It's almost unbelievable, but I received a cancellation for this very room half an hour ago, for the following dates: Saturday, February 12 to Saturday, February 26. Would that fit?"

That was the sign for Natalie. Room 408 boasted a great view of the beautiful park and the distant Silvretta Glacier. The room had just become vacant. Natalie had learned over the past decades that it was wise to pay attention to such so-called coincidences. She booked.

Part One - Hotel Silvretta

1

Stefanos' smiling, sunburned, wrinkled face slowly dissolved in the fog rising from the sea.

Natalie woke up in her warm bed. It smelled like pinewood in the room. She turned on her back to catch the first rays of sunshine that illuminated room 408 through the open curtains. Christian Erpenbeck, the charming owner and director of the hotel, had said this was the room with the most spectacular view, because it looked directly out to the Silvretta Park and the white gleam of the glacier in the background.

Uncle Stefanos was more than an uncle to Natalie. He was a source of wisdom, kindness and deep understanding. What did he say in her dream? Stefanos had died almost 20 years ago – and yet he was always present like a gentle, whispering mist. Even now, Natalie carried his memory and her love for him as a cherished treasure in her heart.

Slowly and a bit foggy, the memory of a few shreds of the dream came back. Stefanos had held her hands. . . they were somewhere on the island of Nisyros, where he lived. . . at the top of the hill near Nikia. She saw his ocean-blue eyes with the penetrating, heart-warming and soul-searching gaze. And she heard his dark, soft voice:

"Agapiméni mou, my sweetheart. In this universe, nothing and no one is ever lost. Look beyond the images you see. Think deeper than your thoughts. Listen beyond the words you hear. Remember what you have always known. . . . "

That's when the dream ended. Stefanos had written those same words to her in a letter countless years ago. Natalie couldn't remember what else he may have said. The bright winter sun bathed the room in soft golden light, and Natalie got up. She opened the window wide to let in the crisp mountain air. Snow sparkled on the conifers and roof tops. The smell of wood fire, first-class hotel cuisine and new snow wafted in. That's how Klosters had always smelled, so wonderfully fresh and homely at the same time.

At the far back, at the end of the valley, the Silvretta glacier shimmered brightly. The fir trees wore their glittering winter dress under a kitschy blue sky. Welcome to Klosters!

Over strong coffee and crispy croissants in the breakfast room, also dressed in pinewood, Natalie looked at the brochure of the 800th anniversary of Klosters. Title: Walserstolz und Weltgeschichten. There was so much to see and experience this year. To learn about the rich history and epic stories. They had made an exceptional effort, the Klosters citizens, putting together something truly special.

But today Natalie was not going to join the buzz. She wanted to be alone. In a few days, on February 18th, was the demo show of the ski schools on Selfranga. She thought she might want to see that. Today she considered going to Monbiel. The remotest village in the

Prättigau was an old Walser settlement and the actual access to the impressive Silvretta mountain range.

Back in the hotel room, she meant to put on her warm winter clothes right away, but her gaze wandered to one of Roman's notebooks, which lay open on the pine bedside table. He had written down his reflections, thoughts and even a few poems in these little brown-beige notebooks, sometimes with pencil or in black ink. Natalie sat down on the bed and began to read:

14 February 1968

There are things that occupy me in a way that I can no longer write. Things that are so banal, they displace my dreams. And yet things that make up life. Because that's what the order wants. And that's what's bothering me: our order, our scheme. The musts and the shoulds. The rules of society. And society itself.

It's the same thing over and over and over again. It's starting to feel so worn out and tiring.

This eternal recurrence of my dissatisfaction with the life I lead. The desire to escape is often overwhelming. I've written about it a hundred times. I'm weary of holding on to the same flat and colourless thoughts.

It's after midnight and I should get some sleep. So that I can go back to work tomorrow. In this beautiful, luxurious hotel. For what? Again, a pattern: you go to work. For others. You make money. That's actually already enough. But then comes the thinking of the others. It hurts to listen to their empty words. It disgusts me when they only talk about cars, fashion, sex, money, parties, prestige, television and progress.

And there I am. Right in the middle. Mercilessly dragged along. No, that's not true: I allowed it. I dream of getting away. Not just since today. I dream of freedom. Of breaking these shackles. Get out of this country, these stale rules. When I was a child, the world seemed pure and bright to me. What happened?

Ah, but I don't act. I'm standing still. I won't open the door. That's what confuses me, puzzles me. And I can only solve this by writing. Because this is the only way I recognize what's bothering me.

Then I remember that I am who I am. That I have a choice. That all I have to do is kick the door open. And that I can. And I will. When I stand alone in the darkness under the infinity of the starry sky – then I know that anything is possible.

Not once had Natalie heard Roman talk like this. Almost desperate, even angry. He had never revealed this side to her. She remained seated on the comfortable bed. The pictures of her teenage years began to roll in front of her eyes like an old film. Slow and yet insistent, in intense technicolor colours.

2

December 1968

Natalie, her sister Margo and their parents had finally arrived in Klosters after a five-hour drive. Papi's fancy
Chrysler had hesitantly but steadily plowed through the
snow, and now it was standing in a parking lot in front of
the Hotel Silvretta. Natalie's heart made little summer-
saults like always when they were finally there. For eight
years, the Steiners had been visiting the picturesque
Klosters – several times every year – and of course,
every time they stayed at the Silvretta.

According to Papi, the Hotel Silvretta was founded in
1870 by Josias Mattli. At the beginning of the 20th century, extensive extensions and conversions were carried
out. The striking arcades at the front of the Silvretta,
through which Natalie had just entered the hotel, were
also built at that time.

Behind the counter in the wonderfully warm, cozy

entrance stood – as always – the concierge, Mr. Manser. Natalie loved the small, round man with the spare grey-black hair and the thin black moustache. He was wearing a beautiful old-fashioned gold pocket watch with a chain in the small left pocket of his vest. Like in a movie, Natalie thought. Mr. Manser had a habit of smiling incessantly when talking to a guest.

"Natalie, Margo, it's already 6:18 pm. Go to your room, unpack and change, dinner is at 7:00." That was Mama's voice, Denise Steiner. Tall, slim, blond, elegant and strict. Papi, Dr. Kurt Steiner, could also be strict, but he was often lenient with his daughters. And the twinkle in his grey eyes revealed his true nature.

"I don't know what to wear, Margo. . . " Natalie was standing in front of her unpacked suitcase. Margo was two years younger than Natalie; she had gold-blonde hair that fell softly to her shoulders, light eyes and a sweet rounded nose. Natalie always felt herself to be a little rough and more robust than her sister, in every way. She looked at herself in the big mirror:

"Margo, my hair is too wild with these curls and I think

I've gained weight. "

"Yes, yes, Natalie, get ready now. Mama will be wait-ing." Margo was Mama's favourite.

Mama and Papi sat down in the bar after dinner, where it smelled of cigarette smoke and leather, and the piano player played his everlasting, cheesy songs – at least to Natalie's ears.

"Have you seen the new young waiter, Margo? He is sooo handsome! That mischievous smile from his hazel-brown eyes. . . "

"Well, really, Natalie, he's way too young for you!"

"Maybe. . . But he's cute and interesting, somehow dif-ferent. Hmm. . . Actually, I think he's older. I'll have to tell Maja. "

Natalie and Margo had arrived at the games room, where the young guests usually met in the evening. Even the young Roccos, the two daughters and the son of the owners of the Silvretta, were often there. There were pin-ball machines and a 'Töggelikasten' and – very im-portant! – a jukebox.

Bee Gees and Beatles, CCR and Rolling Stones, Procol Harum and Donovan, Beach Boys and Moody Blues. It was a great selection of pop music. Margo and Natalie loved the Bee Gees – Massachusetts, To Love Somebody, First of May, and all the other songs, too. Natalie's favourite piece, however, was Scott McKenzie's San Francisco. That's where she wanted to go, where the Hippies were. But she knew her parents would never allow it.

3

At the beginning of June of the following year, Mama announced:

"This summer we are going to Klosters for three weeks only. Uncle Stefanos has invited us to Nisyros. And in case you don't know where this is, it's a small island in the Mediterranean near the island of Kos, both of which belong to the Greek Dodecanese."

"Who on Earth is Uncle Stefanos?" asked Natalie.

"Uncle Stefanos is one of Papi's best friends. He's not related by blood, but he's still family. You'll love him, Natalie. He's very natural and a free spirit like you."

"And me?" Margo seemed to feel left out.

"You'll like him too, Margo. Uncle Stefanos loves children and he tells wonderful stories."

Natalie actually wanted to spend six weeks at the Silvretta in Klosters. She had found out that Roman, the handsome young waiter, would be there again this summer. Her 17th birthday was on June 12. Of course, the school holidays would not yet have started. But she could conceivably celebrate again in Klosters in July.

"But Mama, why are we on a Greek island with an uncle we don't even know?" Natalie was a bit upset.

"Natalie, this year we are going to visit Uncle Stefanos. Period. Papi finally wanted to go to Nisyros again. And anyway, we are going to Klosters for a few weeks after."

Natalie muttered something and Margo shook her head. Sometimes it was really hard to have to do what your parents wanted.

* * *

Denise Steiner, wife of the renowned and respected lawyer Dr. Kurt Steiner in Basel, had imagined the trip to Nisyros without her daughters. Kurt, however, insisted: "Natalie and Margo must come along; especially because Stefanos had expressly asked for it."

Denise had no choice but to accept Kurt's will as graciously as she could manage, which was not easy for her. She could imagine that it might be a challenge for two teenagers like Natalie and Margo to spend three weeks on a small Greek island with a quirky, old fellow. And then who had to make peace? Yes, she, Denise, the mother. However, she did not speak to Kurt about her thoughts.

Denise had met Kurt at the university in Basel. He was tall and slender, had dark, short hair and a charming smile. He was 25 and was already finishing his law degree. Denise, age 19, was deeply impressed. She came from humble backgrounds, mother and father often quarrelled, and Denise wanted nothing but to get away from home. She was lucky: Kurt found her adorable, and proposed marriage after six months of holding hands. To her great joy and before she was 20 she became Mrs. Dr. Steiner.

* * *

Natalie and Maja were on the phone:

"Maja, you won't believe this. We're going to Klosters for only three weeks. And the other three weeks we're going to a Greek island, I think it's called Nissiros, or something, where an old friend of Papi's lives. What a drag!"

"Are you losing your mind, Natalie? That's great! Greek island! That's a hundred times better than always tramping around in a mountain village!"

"And what about Roman, Maja? I'll never really get to know him in just a few weeks."

"Natalie, you'll see him again in any case. Life will bring you exactly what's right for you. You know that."

"Yes, yes. . . Hesse and his poem Stufen, isn't it: '. . . And there is magic in every beginning that protects us and helps us to live. . . '"

"Exactly, Natalie. Ha, by the way, can I come with you?"

"What? Now you're going nuts, Maja. Mama would never allow that."

"You could at least ask her, right?! No, wait, ask your Papi, he's more understanding in such things."

"OK, Maja, great idea. I will. Ciao, ciao, I'll call you later. No, it'll be too late. I'll see you tomorrow at school. Nighty night."

"Sweet dreams, Natalie."

Maja Rim, Natalie's long-time and long-haired best friend, was already excited. She had a strong sense that the trip to Nisyros would work. Maja always relied on her gut feeling. Her mother, who came from Southampton, England, left her this legacy long before she died.

4

Natalie was still sitting on her bed in the cozy room at the hotel. She had brushed her teeth, but she had not gotten much further in the meantime.

It's really crazy, she thought, *how the memories of all those years from so long ago come back to life here at the Silvretta. Maja would say 'uncanny'.*

The Postauto to Monbiel was ready to leave from Klosters station when Natalie, dressed in a dark blue ski suit, boarded with a leather backpack and snowshoes. Only a few seats were occupied, so she sat down by the window. She took off her woolen gloves, removed the knitted black headband and shook her shoulder-length, grey-white hair.

Natalie watched the sun-kissed snowy landscape, the dark brown cattle stables of the Walser, the Gadä, on the hills and the beloved, shiny white mountain peaks pass by. Her thoughts, however, wandered back to the summer of 1969, when she, Margo and her parents arrived in Klosters after their holiday on Nisyros. Of course, Papi had made it happen and Maja had actually been allowed to come to the Greek island. Papi was just great.

* * *

On Saturday, July 26, 1969, the Steiner family arrived punctually at 7 pm in the dining room of the Hotel Silvretta. As always, the tables were set with white, ironed and starched tablecloths and napkins, plus a slim silver vase with a rose, sparkling glasses and silver cutlery.

Everything is so chic and elegant and somehow stiff, Natalie thought, *on Nisyros with Uncle Stefanos it was really simpler and more natural. You also didn't have to change your clothes all the time. . . .* The thought never came to an end. Natalie had discovered Roman. She kicked Margo's leg underneath the table, and her sister rolled her eyes.

Roman Camenisch, like all waiters, was dressed in black and white. The jacket stretched slightly over his broad shoulders, and the trousers were rather too short for his long legs. He had also seen Natalie. With a gesture that was typical of him, he ran the fingers of his left hand through his rather long, chestnut-brown hair.

This girl is different from the others, he mused. *This time I'm going to get to know her.*

In his tiny room on the top story, just beneath the roof of the Silvretta, Roman lay stretched out on his bed after work. He had a small notebook in his left hand and a pencil in the other. He liked to make notes of his experiences and thoughts; from time to time he also wrote poems. Whenever he moved to a different place, his notebooks went with him.

July 26, 1969
Life is not just a series of coincidences. On the contrary. Life plays its cards, and it's up to us what we do with it.
The Queen of Hearts arrived today. How I'm

going to get closer to her, I don't know yet. Every-
thing's open. Even though she comes from a wealthy
family and from the city, and I'm a mountain boy work-
ing as a waiter.

As Hesse said: And there is magic in every beginning...

* * *

Meanwhile, Natalie and Margo had also arrived in their room at the back of the Kurhaus on the third floor.

"This room is terribly spartan, don't you think, Natalie?" Margo said. "The one Mama and Papi have is so much nicer."

"Yes, that's right, but I really don't care. – Margo, did you notice: Roman has grown up, so to speak, in the six months we haven't seen him. Tall and broad-shouldered, even a small moustache and a kind of Jesus beard, a bit Hippie-like. And, you know, his eyes are so deep and intense. . . "

"Don't get your hopes up, Natalie. Mama won't like to see you hanging out with a waiter."

"Margo, I don't really care about that either! Now sleep well."

Before falling asleep, Natalie thought of the conversation she, Maja and Stefanos had had on a wonderfully warm evening on the island. Stefanos greeted them with: "Kalispera, ómorfes kyríes. Good evening, beautiful ladies."

Stefanos was on a roll, and his thick, silvery moustache seemed to bounce. He spoke of love:

"My two beautiful, bright young ladies! For you in your youth love is always related to a young man. But that is not what I call love. That is being in love. Love is an inner attitude. It radiates from the inside of a person outward. It is not egotistical or possessive. It is benevolent and compassionate. It is utterly responsible and unselfish."

Oh my, that was the beginning of a discussion that hissed back and forth. Maja, of course, was fire and flame. Natalie was still unsure today what had come out of it. And she had not fully understood Stefanos' explanation one way or the other. He was a really quirky and rather eccentric guy. Stefanos knew a lot, cooked well, understood young people and always had a smile on his wrinkled face.

5

July 29, 1969 - full moon. Roman knew that. And he was off that Tuesday. Yesterday he had briefly spoken to Natalie in the park, where he had been serving drinks to some of the hotel guests, who were reclining on the colourful lawn chairs. Natalie had actually agreed to meet him tonight after dinner outside the hotel.

Even before their evening meal, Natalie had convinced her sister: "Well, Margo, we'll tell Mama and Papi that we're going to the games room as usual. But I'm going to leave right away and meet Roman outside. You're not alone, the Roccos and the others will be there too. And I'll be back soon. OK?"

"Okay, darling sister. But don't take too long."

It was not dark outside – Maja would call it 'moon-bright'. Natalie immediately saw Roman across the street. How tall he was. Faded jeans and a flowered shirt, Hippie-like. She felt a little fluttery, insecure somehow. It wasn't just the butterflies in her belly, there was something like a premonition. A vague, fleeting moment of knowing what she did not know.

"Hi Natalie. Come on, let's go a little further into the park where there aren't so many lights. It's full moon, we can see enough."

Roman took her hand as if they had always walked together like this.

The grass in the Silvretta park was dark green, the trees cast long shadows, and in the silver moonlight even the tennis courts seemed to have something mystical about them. It smelled of sun-warmed meadows and fresh mountain air.

Natalie was not sure she wasn't dreaming. Roman's hand still held hers, and she felt the warmth of his fingers with every cell of her skin.

Roman, however, was aware that Natalie seemed a little shy. He would not have expected that of her, thus far she had appeared rather self-confident and sometimes even arrogant. He let go of her hand.

"Come, let's sit under this Beech tree. Here's my jacket, so that your pretty dress doesn't get stained with grass. Tell me, Natalie, about your dreams, thoughts, ideas."

Natalie had to admit to herself that she was confused: *There I am sitting next to this big, charming Hippie waiter in the Silvretta Park – and he asks me about my dreams?! I've never experienced anything like this before. Never. And then there's this sonorous voice with the rolling Grisons dialect. It's crazy.*

"Roman, that's an unusual invitation, really. I. . . I don't know what to say. . . "

"Okay, I'll start, Natalie. In short: I come from Sent in the Lower Engadin. I have dreams that have nothing to do with hotels and waiter jobs. But somehow I have to make money to make my dreams come true. Anyway. . .

"My dreams: I want to go to Canada for a long time. Or New Zealand. I wish I could be at the Woodstock Rock

Festival next month. I wish there were no wars like the vile, cruel war in Vietnam. I hope that the Hippie movement will continue and that there will be more peace in the world. Better flowers in your hair and barefoot than with a machine gun in the trench. . ."

Roman was quiet. With his left hand he stroked his almost shoulder-length hair. His high cheekbones, his not too dense moustache and the small beard on his chin were dimly lit by the moon.

Natalie was also silent. But her thoughts were alive: *My God, he looks like a total Hippie in that light. And besides, almost as I would have imagined Jesus. What kind of man is that? And he speaks of a peaceful world and distant lands. And Woodstock! And me? I'm stupidly speechless. It won't work this way; I have to speak up...*

"Woodstock. Wow, Roman. Yes, that would be something. I would love to experience that. Hopefully they will at least broadcast it on TV. You know, my parents would never allow me to go to a festival. School first, holidays with mom and dad, then university or some other education. And then when I'm 25 and independent of them, it's too late. . . And yes, wars are terrible. I wish there weren't any."

Natalie looked at Roman, who returned her gaze with a slightly crooked and stunning smile.

"Well, then we two think alike, Natalie. Great. And by the way: I love mountains, forests, stars, oceans, animals, Hermann Hesse – ah yes, and of course the moon. Isn't it incredible that this round, bright satellite of our Earth was stepped on by humans eight days ago?! Just unbelievable."

"Yes, that's what it is - unbelievable. We're going to the moon, but we can't stop wars. And the people in leadership who might be able to do something about it are murdered – like John F. Kennedy, Martin Luther King, and Bobby Kennedy. I don't know, but I think we're living in crazy times, Roman. So, there's only one thing for me: I have to finish school and look for a job that makes sense.

– Ugh, we've been gone for over an hour now. I have to go back, Roman. My sister's waiting for me."

6

February 2022

The Postauto had arrived in Monbiel, and Natalie surfaced from her memories as if she were reliving those
moments. *It is inconceivable that the world has not really
changed in those 52 years,* she thought. *Ah, but I am
here now, in my beloved glittering white mountain world.
And this is almost like a miracle.*

It was cold, at least -15 Celsius. For Natalie it felt re-
freshing, alive. And she knew that by the time she
reached Alp Garfiun the sun would be shining. She was
also thinking of walking to the Circle of Stones in the next
few days, which stood in a bend of the young river Landquart, not far from the confluence of the crystalline glacier fed creeks Vereinabach and Verstanclabach. For that
she definitely needed her snowshoes. This was no
cleared nor trodden path in the winter. But not today. It
was too early.

Natalie had rented a pair of modern style snowshoes at Sport Andrist. After having walked from Monbiel just past the Rütistall she put them on and continued via Schwendi to Alp Garfiun. The snow was deep, the sun already strong, and after only ten minutes of hiking uphill she took her jacket off and fastened it onto the packsack.

Phew. I must have truly gotten older…, Natalie thought a bit dejectedly after the first half hour of snow-shoeing. She was out of breath – or close to, and her heart was beating faster than she was used to. She had laboured up to a wooden bench above Alp Garfiun. She gratefully sat down and savoured the bright sunshine, the sparkling snow, the view of snowy peaks and the crisp mountain air. She thought she could smell the scent of the fir trees in the warmth of the sun. She smiled, think-ing of what Maja would say: "How can it get any better than this?"

Natalie closed her eyes. Like in a familiar dream, she was already back in the summer of 1969. A line of Bryan Adam's song 'In the Summer of '69' swirled through her mind: … *those were the best days of my life.*

August 1969

After their first meeting in the Silvretta Park, Natalie and Roman saw each other as often as possible, when parents are in the way. Margo was quite content to spend a few hours with other girls who were also staying at the hotel. Although Denise Steiner was usually busy with her blonde and slim girlfriend Dora, she began to notice that Natalie appeared to be nowhere. Papi was often playing tennis on the courts in the park or he had some business to discuss with his friend and hotel owner Giorgio Rocco. Natalie liked Giorgio Rocco. He was a bit stocky, always impeccably dressed, and he loved to tell jokes. His intelligent eyes sparkled good-naturedly in his weather-worn face.

August 8 was a bright, radiant summer day. Natalie and Roman drove to Monbiel with their mopeds and on toward Vereinatal. This was no mere ride on a road – they had to cross meadows and creeks, tree roots and rocky parts. Near the confluence of the two glacier creeks Roman veered toward a rolling mountain meadow.

"I don't think I can pass through here with my moped, Roman."

"Come, let's get off the bikes and push them. I'd like to leave the trail here. See, over there, behind the small hill with the triangular rock, there is a stand of several large firs. Nobody will bother us there."

Roman – thinking of everything – had brought a blanket and two bottles of Coke. Natalie leaned comfortably on Roman as if they had been long-time friends. He gently stroked her hands with his long fingers. Tiny golden stars twinkled in his hazel eyes: "I'm going to tell you a story now, one of the myths of this area. It's the story of Vereina and Silvretta, two sisters." What he was thinking, though: *I really want to kiss her... But now I have to tell her the story first.*

Natalie snuggled up to him, her head on his shoulder, and listened to his warm, resonant voice. At the start of their excursion she had felt some trepidation, a kind of unusual insecurity. Her adventurous spirit and the fact that she was falling in love with Roman had dispersed those feelings. She trusted him. Trust - this was another teaching Stefanos had imparted:

"We humans cannot control life. We can, however, learn to adapt to any situations, even if they are uncomfortable. We can learn to trust life – or that which exists beyond life. I heard it said that once upon a time there was a Zen master, who proclaimed: 'The master trusts the trustworthy; and she trusts the untrustworthy.'"

Roman began:

"When I was a small boy, my father, Gion, told me the myth about the Silvretta mountain range. He died just before I turned eight... ten years ago, already..."

He was silent for a moment. As he ran his left hand through his hair, he glimpsed himself as a boy in the small cold bedroom of his parents' wooden home, waiting for his dad's story. Natalie saw the faraway look in his eyes and felt something like distant grief, but he smiled his little mischievous smile and continued:

43

"Well, then, the story of the myth of Vereina and Silvretta:

"A long, long time ago there came a mysterious nobleman called Alfonso Baretto from a land far to the South. There were whispered rumours among the mountain people that he had been banned from Italy, the land of his fathers. The contemporary nobles there would not tolerate Baretto's honesty and open-mindedness. Thus he was seeking refuge in the quiet and peaceful world of the Alps, far away from people.

"High above the valley he found a large, dry cave in the vicinity of Stutzalp, which he set up as a comfortable home. He lived there with his beloved daughters, Silvretta and Vereina. They lived on roots and berries and the abundant yield of their hunts, happy with their simple and yet rich life. Even until today this cave is called Baretto Balma.

"After many years, Baretto slowly befriended a few hunters and shepherds that he met on his forays. He sometimes visited them in their alpine huts and began to reconcile himself with humanity. Then one day he even took his blossoming daughters all the way to Klosters to participate in the festivities of the rural population.

"Baretto died peacefully at an advanced age. The two daughters buried him in the cave and sprinkled the grave with sweet-scented mountain herbs.

"Not long after, Silvretta began to long for her old, milder home in Italy, and bid farewell to her sister. She travelled over the massive mountain range to the South, and ever since, these mountains have been called Silvretta.

"Vereina, however, stayed for a good long while, mysteriously wandering through valleys and mountains. The people from Monbiel were very fond of her sociable personality despite her wild hair and outlandish ways. When she was last seen, she stood on top of one of the mountains that afforded a far and fair view over the Prättigau. She had spread her arms wide in blessing, and it was told that she called out across the expanse:

"'*Farewell, you beloved land; and to you, happy villages, whom my eye sees for the last time today, I give my valleys with their fertile pastures.*' Thus, Vereina took her leave from this land. At least this is what some say. There are others who claim that Vereina still wanders over the glaciers and lives with the chamois far back in the Vereinatal.

"And here we are, you and I, Natalie, at the entrance to the mysterious and beautiful Vereinatal. My most cherished valley of all."

Natalie had let herself be carried so far away by Roman's soft, deep voice and this old myth that it took a moment to find her way back into the world of here and now. And here they were, in Roman's most loved valley, where the air was scented with mountain thyme and fir. Where she could hear the young river Landquart softly murmur her song in the background. And where life felt so simple and right and filled with a sense of meaning.

"I want to stay here, Roman. I never want to leave again. Just like in the myth: through a simple life we will find contentment and happiness."

Roman held Natalie in his arms and whispered in her ear: "I wish with all my heart that we could stay here, Natalie…" He turned her head gently so that their faces were almost touching. And finally he kissed her, tenderly and softly at first, until her passion began to burst into flame.

7

"Margo, do you have any idea where Natalie is? Dinner is in an hour and I haven't seen her anywhere." Denise was at the end of her patience.

"Margo!" Louder now. "Where is Natalie?"

Margo tried in vain to avoid giving an answer. It had been a dazzling summer afternoon in the park, and she had enjoyed the company of another girl, Andrea with the flaming red hair. They had been lounging on the lawn chairs near the tennis courts, where Papi and Andrea's dad were playing. The waiter had brought tall glasses of Coke with ice cubes and a slice of orange – heavenly.

"Mama, the only thing I know is that she drove away with the moped. I'm sure she'll be back soon."

Denise marched back and forth in the girls' hotel room, her cheeks were slightly flushed. Margo thought: *Thank goodness she's not wearing her high heels.*

The door flew open. Natalie. Her hair all tangled, her jeans streaked with dirt and her face beautifully kissed by the sun. "Something wrong?"

Denise's stare spoke volumes. Natalie was aware of how she looked and what her mother thought of it.

"I was in the Vereinatal with the moped. It's just gorgeous there. Sorry I'm late."

Denise composed herself with remarkable effort: "I'm glad you're safely back, Natalie. Wash up, change into evening clothes. I want to see you 15 minutes before dinner in my room." Denise opened the door and was gone.

"Shit. I am 17 and she treats me as if I was still in diapers. – Margo, what did you tell Mama?"

"Nothing, Natalie. Just that you had left on your moped. I swear, absolutely nothing else."

"OK, super. Thank you, Margo! Well, I suppose I better hurry and get cleaned up so that I can listen to the lecture before dinner..."

* * *

Roman was sitting on his huge bed in his tiny room. Actually, perhaps the bed wasn't really that large, but it felt like that to him because the space was so small.

His notebook was lying beside him, and the pencil was waiting to be useful.

> *August 8, 1969*
> *What did I write here a few days ago? 'Life is not just a series of coincidences. It plays its cards...' Yes, and then the Queen of Hearts arrived. And today we didn't only kiss each other, we were also close in our souls. It is different with Natalie. I wish I could find the words...*
>
> *Who said this: 'When we don't write we are not truly awake.'? – Ah, yes, that was Pascal Mercier. And isn't it frankly like this? If we just live (or perhaps stumble) through the day, we are not really here. When I write down my thoughts, feelings, experiences, I perceive a much deeper substance*

in my life. An essence I would not be able to grasp otherwise.

Well, now, Natalie. She will run into difficulties with her parents. Or, rather, more with her mother than her father. Kurt Steiner appears to be fairly open-minded, perhaps even a bit of an incognito adventurer. He told me once that he had lived in the USA. That would have opened his horizon.

I'm not quite sure yet what Natalie means for or in my life. Yet she definitely means something to me. Which I cannot honestly say about most girls I've ever met, as nice as they were. The Queen of Hearts has appeared. I think I remember a poem by a young woman, who was from Basel, yet also from England. What was her name… ah, got it: Maja Rim.

And I even have that poem here in one of my old notebooks:

Queen of Hearts

It struck me again today
like lightning hitting full target
that the universe is dealing the cards
and it is up to me
to decide which one to play

The queen of hearts
she who governs the life of all lovers
cannot beat the ace
I am left with a losing card
and the option to fold

To end the game right here and now
would be the choice of the wise
but still, the queen of hearts whispers:
better to have loved and lost
than not have loved at all

She knows that
in the end,
when all else falls away
love is all that matters

So I play the queen of hearts
and I know I have won

8

Natalie was finally allowed to use the phone in her parents' bedroom after the lecture and a drawn-out dinner. She had to admit that the meal had been delicious as always – shrimp cocktail, tenderloin Wellington and coupe Danmark for dessert. Now it was time to call Maja.

"Maja, thank goodness you're home! It's unbelievable, really. Roman is such an exceptional man, and everything is going so well, and it doesn't actually make sense, but it's still important, and life plays other cards than we expect, and Mama is beside herself, and…"

Maja stopped her: "Woah, Natalie, slow down, breathe. Now start at the beginning, ok?!"

Natalie told Maja about the trip with the mopeds, about the Vereinatal and its myths, their first kiss and caresses in the mountain meadow, the cow bells in the distance, the murmuring of the Landquart and the aromatic scent of mountain thyme.

"Maja, I cannot explain it, but there is something about Roman that feels so right, so familiar even – as if we had known each other for eons. He is just one year older than I am, but I swear he must have as much life experience as Papi. Not only because of what happened in his life – his dad died young and Roman has been looking after his mom ever since – but also how he thinks, what he knows, the books he has read. And yet, he is also young, well, kind of like a Hippie.

"He and I, we could build ourselves a life somewhere in the wilderness, grow our own food on our homestead, make our own furniture, help others, live peacefully and purposefully… But as you can guess: my parents have already activated the full stop button. Of course, Mama was the instigator, but Papi has to go along with it, unless he's willing to risk a marriage crisis. We are leaving in two days! Can you imagine!?"

"Oh shit, Natalie! I mean, darn… What are we going to do? Write – you have to write to Roman. And I'm sure you will be going back to Klosters in the fall and for

Christmas. And perhaps you could talk to Stefanos. Hmm, no, that won't work, he doesn't have a phone on Nisyros. You can write to him, too. There is always a solution, for everything. Call me when you're back home in Basel! Take it easy, girl!"

When Natalie went to bed, she felt much calmer. In her hand she held the braided leather bracelet, adorned with colourful glass beads, that Roman had given her today. "A late birthday present", he said, gracing her with his slightly crooked and mischievous smile that undid her every time. The whole afternoon had been a gift for Natalie, and she thanked the gods for it in silence. She was absolutely not religious, but today she felt that there was so much in life that was inexplicable – perhaps there was some divine plan after all.

Life is a mystery, she thought, *and that is as it needs to be. We don't have to explain everything – it is impossible for us to do so, anyway. Stefanos and Maja would agree...* With those thoughts drifting through her mind like a mist and with the leather bracelet in her hand she fell asleep.

In her dream, Natalie was once more on Nisyros, the volcanic island in the Aegean Sea. Natalie, Maja and Margo were sitting on white wooden chairs with airy rattan seats in front of Stefanos' picturesque house in Nikia. The deep pink bougainvillea enfolded the house in a glowing embrace. The view from the house over the insanely steep slopes down to the azure sea was utterly breathtaking. Stefanos' eyes had the same colour and they sparkled as he told them the myth of the creation of the island:

Thousands and thousands of years ago there raged a great battle in this part of the Mare Internum (as the Romans used to call it) between the gods and the giants. The god of the sea, Poseidon, was chasing the giant Polyvotis, who loved to wage havoc where he could. Poseidon hunted the giant all the way to the island Kos, cut off a part of it and threw it at Polyvotis, who sank to the bottom of the Aegean Sea for eternity.

This chunk of rock that holds Polyvotis down to the bottom of the sea is Nisyros. It is told that the eruptions of the volcano are nothing but the angry breaths of the giant, who desperately tries to free himself from the island.

As you know, this whole island is a volcano. One of the craters – and you can climb down into it because its small steam eruptions are not dangerous – is called Stefanos...

Stefanos' uproariously resounding and happy laughter reverberated in Natalie's dream into the far distance, where the sea and the horizon met in unequivocal unity.

9

Stefanos had a steaming cup of sage tea in front of him on the small, scrubbed wooden table in his blue and white house in Nikia on the island of Nisyros. Most tourists who visited Nikia could not understand why anyone would want to live in a tiny, quaint and antiquated village on top of a mountain on a volcanic island. The whole island was small – only about 42 km^2 –, extremely dry, with hair-raisingly steep, terraced slopes only goats could negotiate. And then there was the dormant but not extinct volcano.

The view from Nikia down to the azure blue and turquoise Aegean Sea was breathtaking. By the sea's edge stood Mandraki, the capital, with whitewashed houses sporting blue trimmed doors and window shutters. The cafés, pubs and inns along the shore were popular points of attraction, even more so than the few natural sandy beaches outside the city. Nisyros counted barely 800 inhabitants, about 40 of them lived in Nikia.

Stefanos loved his quiet and his solitude way up on the mountain. Decades ago, he had studied botany in Berkeley, and throughout his life he had worked in various botanical gardens. Plants of all kinds were his best friends, his family. Around his house here in Nikia he tended lovingly to his many flowers and the extensive herb garden.

His deeply suntanned skin folded into a multitude of wrinkles as he read and smiled at Natalie's letter. *What a sweet, crazy girl,* he chuckled; *it would be so good for her to live a year or so with me up here.* He fondly remembered the few weeks that the Steiners and Natalie's friend Maja spent at his home only last month. He had felt a connection with Natalie as if he was truly her uncle.

She is open-minded and wears her heart on her sleeve unlike most of the girls at her age, he mused. *She is interested in almost everything, she has an adventurous spirit – and sometimes she's downright sassy. I like that in her.*

Stefanos had enjoyed the many conversations, sometimes turned arguments, with Natalie and Maja. The girls
brought a fresh, lively wind into his house. For Margo he
had an inexhaustible stash of stories from Greek mythology, which he told her at bedtime to her utter delight.
Later in the evenings, Stefanos and Kurt would sit outside, a bottle of Ouzo on the table, and reminisce about
their days at the University of Berkely. Denise liked to listen to their memories, but Stefanos was sure that she
would have preferred being in a classy hotel with musical
entertainment.

Natalie's letter needed a reply. Stefanos found great
pleasure in writing on handmade paper with his old,
sturdy fountain pen:

September 1969

Agapiméni mou!
Many thanks for your trust and honesty, dear Na-
talie. I feel truly honoured.

Yes, it is very important and often wise to listen to our inner voice. Sometimes, however, we mistake it for what our mind wants. Would you be able to take a week or so away from the buzz of your life in Basel to really listen to the whispers of your soul?

Do you remember when you, Maja and I visited the small chapel of Agios Ionnis Theologos on the hill outside of Nikia? I had asked you two to sit in silence for an hour and to watch what was happening in your thoughts – and to especially pay attention to what surfaced behind your thoughts. This is what I suggest to you now – if possible, daily for a few hours and for a whole week. You will recognize that the answers to your queries – how to go on with Roman, what to study, and how to come to an agreement with your parents – are already there.

One of my most cherished thinkers, Kahlil Gibran, is quoted to have said: 'And think not that you can guide the course of love. For love, if it finds you worthy, shall guide your course.'

My thoughts are with you, Natalie. May you find your way. When I can, I will always stand by your side.

Is to epanidín! Until we meet again!

Stefanos

PS: Do not forget to talk with your Papi alone. He has a great open heart.
PPS: In Maja you have a true and wonderful friend; she is there for you.

10

Roman knew it: Natalie's parents were being difficult, especially her mother. Phoning Natalie was out of the question. Telling her in letters about his plans and his genuine love for her, was all he could do for now. Natalie wrote quite often despite being busy at school. And now, her mother had signed her up for lessons in advanced English in the evenings.

That's just as well, thought Roman, *the better her English, the easier it will be to obtain a visa and to immigrate to any English-speaking country.*

Summer season in Klosters was almost over, it was already mid-October. Roman was going home to see his mother in the lower Engadin. And in December the whole winter circus was starting up again. He was going to work at Hotel Silvretta once more, and the Steiner family would be there for Christmas. With Natalie.

Roman was actually looking forward to see his best friend again soon: Dumeng was a mountain farmer's son from Sent, copper-blond, tall and skinny, with bright, alert eyes. They had gone to school together in that small, cold schoolhouse in Sent, they had been skiing and hiking together in the far reaches of the surrounding mountains. Once in a while they got drunk together in the village pub, and sometimes they exchanged girls. But most important of all, they were always there for each other.

Dumeng had to work on his parents' farm, there was no other choice. Before Roman had left for work at Hotel Silvretta in Klosters, he helped Dumeng whenever possible to milk the cows and muck out the barns. They both knew with absolute certainty that they could depend on each other, even though they might be hundreds of miles apart.

On this particular Saturday, like he often did in the evenings, Roman was sitting on the big, soft bed in his cramped room under the eaves of Hotel Silvretta, notebook at the ready:

October 18, 1968

*There's not much happening anymore here in the
hotel. Just one more week – full moon, too! – and
I can finally leave this place. It's quite remarkable
how the upper- class society bothers me more
and more. What is it that makes me shiver when I
see these stylish women, dressed up to the nines
and wearing heavy make-up with their husbands
in tuxedos, who are just waiting to go down to the
Five to Five club to drink their Whisky?*

*I just found out, by the way: The Five to Five
Club, the hidden and confoundingly complex
meeting space of celebrities and VIPs, had been
created in 1955 – and still existed today mostly
because of Giorgio Rocco's (my big boss) commitment. Natalie once told me that the club held
something mystical for her, because her Papi often seemed to mysteriously disappear there. Anyway...*

*Immigrating to another country on another con-
tinent, that's my goal. There must be places on*

this beautiful planet, where wilderness and free-
dom are closer than they are here. Where people
are more real, in a sense, with open hearts and
minds and an awakened spirit. Canada's North,
perhaps? I'll have to talk to Natalie. She under-
stands the way I think and my longing for a life
that is authentic, genuine, down to earth and per-
haps also hard. A life lived with purpose and con-
nection to the Earth and the universe – and there-
fore also closer to what the sages of this world
call spirituality.

On the other hand, spirituality is, of course, just
part of any real life, woven into the mundane and
day-to-day trivia – but we have to see it, feel it,
hear it! Let's add some Rilke to this:

Ah, not to be cut off, not through the slightest
partition shut out from the law of the stars.

Natalie told me about Stefanos, who lives such
a simple, full, rich (in an inner sense) life on this
small Greek island called Nisyros. He must be

one of the unknown wise men of our time.

Hmmm… Perhaps Natalie and I could visit him on our way to Canada or New Zealand… Making plans… How often they are nothing but castles in the sand. Someone said a while ago: 'Whenever humans make plans, the gods are laughing.'

But – the gods played the Queen of Hearts into my hands…

11

That very same evening, Natalie and Maja finally found time to be together and talk about the world and life and the universe. They met at the pub Gifthüttli in the old part of Basel, but it was too loud and smoky in there. The October evening was mild and there seemed to be a joyful lightness in the air. The two friends crossed the Mittlere Brücke arm in arm to the so-called Kleinbasel (little Basel). It took them a while to find a spot amongst the many other adolescents on the shores of the Rhine River.

Natalie looked at Maja, who – with her long, shiny, black hair that fell far below her shoulders and her slightly slanted, dark eyes – looked more Asian than someone from Basel. There was a reason to this: Maja's father was supposedly a sailor from Thailand, with whom Maja's English mom had fallen in love. Sadly, and to Maja's persistent consternation, he was lost at sea long before she was born.

And, of course and as always, Maja smelled deliciously of Patchouli. "Well, Natalie, I can't get over it: Woodstock was absolutely fantastic! It has been a good two months since, but they are still broadcasting many of the songs and even some film clips. Jimi Hendrix, Janis Joplin, Joan Baez, Santana, CCR, Joe Cocker, the list goes on. It galls me even today that I could not be there!"

"Phenomenal, yes, Maja. Just out of this world. Music and rain and mud and hundreds of thousands of young people, who stood up for freedom and peace and love. As you know, my parents would never have allowed me to go to such a huge Hippie fest. Roman would have loved to be there as well…"

"À propos Roman: have you heard from him, Natalie? And by the way, what about Benno? Are you still seeing him?"

The once beautiful river Rhine was flowing sluggishly past the many young people sitting on its banks. Unconcerned and undisturbed by their sorrows and those of the world. The Rhine had its own worries: its waters were polluted by industrial and chemical poisons. Only many decades later would it be cleaned up sufficiently, so that waterfowl, fish and people could swim in it again.

Natalie was looking into the slow-moving brown-green river, unseeing. Her thoughts had wandered to the clear, turquoise waters of the creeks flowing from the glaciers in the upper Prättigau. She finally answered Maja:

"Roman does write often. He is someone who loves to write, to whom writing is more important than many other things. But you know, Maja, it's just not enough. I want to be with him, to share life with him. Love at a distance is frustrating… Benno, yes. He is such a great, cool, kind guy, and we get along really well. But there is something missing from my part."

Benno Guggenheim, student of medicine at the university of Basel, was Natalie's so-called boyfriend: blond, wavy hair and exceptionally brilliant, deep blue eyes. He came from and old, respected family, who were friends with the Steiners. Denise was very fond of him and loved seeing him come and go at their home. Benno was also best friends with Maja's beau Kris.

"By the way, Maja, I received a letter from Stefanos. He mentioned – amongst many other things – that I could best talk to you about Roman. I just had a thought: wouldn't it be something if Stefanos and Roman could meet? What do you think? They could philosophize together endlessly…"

"That's a great idea, Natalie. Stefanos and Roman – the magician and his apprentice…" Maja's laughter was like sparkling wine. And contagious. In the youthful zest for life, the heartaches and the horrors of the world were momentarily forgotten.

"So, Maja, Stefanos suggested that I sit in complete silence for a few hours a day to listen to what is going on within me. So that I may find my path, my way in every sense of the word, especially also because of Roman. Maja, I cannot just sit down and do nothing for a few hours a day."

Barely moving her head sideways, Maja looked at her friend through her thick, dark lashes. She knew very well that Natalie did not have the patience to sit quietly for hours like a yogi. She also knew that Stefanos was right: a solution could not be found by force.

It is quite clear to me, unfortunately, Maja thought, *that the Steiners, mainly Natalie's mother, would not agree to a relationship with Roman. Which could only mean that Roman and Natalie would have to elope. Crazy, that this kind of prejudice about the lineage and social status of someone would still exist these days..."*

But this was not what Maja said. She told Natalie: "Well, my love, as long as you know what you want, there will be a way. According to what you are saying about Roman – I will have to meet him some day! – he appears to be utterly clear about the direction of his life. And if you are willing to join him in this, fully and with your whole being, then it will work. – So, and now we'll go and have a beer. Benno and Kris are over there; come on Natalie, it's Saturday. Time to relax."

12

Sent, November 30, 1969

My most beloved Natalie
It has been such a long time since we were to-
gether in the meadow near the Engi, close to the
young Landquart and in the shade of the stately fir
trees, talking and dreaming. I love those memories.

Thank you so much for your loving words and news
from your life, so far away from me. And although
writing is one of my passions, as you know, I have
very simply not had the time to reply to your letter.
Please forgive me.

I have been home at my mom's in Sent for several
weeks already. I helped her with the installation of
a new cooking stove – the old one was still wood-
fired. I cleaned and painted the almost grey walls in
the kitchen white; I repaired the lose joints in the at-
tic, and so on. I am also lending a hand daily to

Dumeng – my best, closest friend since I was a boy – on his parents' farm. His parents are growing older, and there is plenty of work with 24 cows, 8 goats, 45 laying hens and the preparations for winter in the extensive vegetable garden and all the outbuildings. What I love most? Mucking out the barns! Second priority is milking the cows.

You're right, Natalie: We have to listen to our inner voice, to our dreams and our intuition. There has to be meaning in this life. There is a reason why you and I met. I have an innate trust that life will always provide us with opportunities to develop ourselves, to grow more and more into what we were born for.

And how I see it, the significance of why we were born and why our paths crossed – besides the love I feel for you – is to pay tribute to life by living it with common sense, integrity, sound ethics, understanding, compassion and love. Might sound a bit over the top and pretentious, I know. But I am convinced that we are capable together of living a natural, healthy, nature-based life.

My preference would be to realize these dreams in Canada. I am actually in the process of applying for immigration. It isn't an easy process; bureaucracy is alive and well all over the world. The simplest way for both of us would, of course, be if we were married...

I know, I know. This is a bit of a shock, sweet Natalie. I'm sorry. Honesty and open-mindedness are also an important part of a relationship, aren't they? Your parents will be against it. Most of all your Mama. I got along quite well with your Papi this past summer. He comes across as a kind-hearted and unbiased man. Perhaps we may need the support of your Uncle Stefanos you were telling me about.

And you, my mountain faery? What do you think? Can you imagine starting a completely new life with me in Canada's wilderness? Do you want to marry me?

So many BIG questions all at once. I know. But if I don't ask them all now, we may not get another chance. When you will be at the Silvretta for Christmas we may not have a lot of opportunities for long conversations and the discussing of plans. Therefore, here is my attempt, albeit not very subtle and not romantic at all. I would have much preferred to kneel in the bright snow by a full moon up on Selfranga to propose this to you…

Christmas/New Year will be hectic at the Silvretta. The hotel is full. Have you heard, by the way, that Josephine Baker will perform at the hotel? Hmmm… do you actually know who she is? An extraordinary lady. Decades ago, she was called the Black Venus. In the golden twenties, she was dancing at certain venues with a skirt made of bananas – and nothing else! As you can imagine, the male audience was roaring.

Originally, Josephine came from extreme poverty in Missouri, USA. Much later, once she became successful, she moved to France and became part of the French Résistance . She earned herself several medals for her achievements. She also supported movements and organizations who opposed racism. Her personal protest manifested in adopting 12 orphans from various cultures – this is what became her famous rainbow family. Fantastic, isn't it!?

I'm sure you will get to hear one of her most famous songs: 'J'ai deux Amours' on New Year's Eve. However, I suspect that this isn't quite that thrilling for you. You might much prefer CCR… Nevertheless, this lady wrote history. Today – at over 60! – she is back on stage because she needs to make money for her large family. Extraordinary, really. Chapeau!

My beloved Natalie, I hope I didn't bore nor upset you with my thoughts, opinions and propositions. We will find time in December (or in January at the latest) to figure out how to get this all rolling. I trust that you agree with my plans – not because they

*are _my_ plans, but because this is also what _you_
want.*

*And so, I am going to bed now, relieved and calmer
because I managed at long last to write to you. Forgive me, my mountain faery, that it took so long.
Just a few more weeks (I think 24 days) until we
see each other again!*

*Remember, you are always in my heart and in my
thoughts.*
Roman

13

Maja was unusually quiet after reading Roman's letter. The two friends were sitting in Maja's digs in Kleinbasel on her bed, which was covered with a stunning, colourful throw from Guatemala. The whole flat was suffused by the subtle and delightful scent of Patchouli. The three slim beeswax candles in the silver candle holder on the small mahogany table were lit.

Maja barely managed a comment: "This is… well… rather surprising. And now?"

Natalie looked into her best friend's beautiful ebony eyes, which gave the impression of an enduring hint of sadness. Neither of them spoke. The silence spread like a thick, heavy cloud in the usually cozy room.

After a while, Maja got up and dropped the letter, which had been written with ink on handmade paper, on her bed. "Now – I am going to pour us both a stiff Gin Tonic. And then you have to get it all out, Natalie!"

Natalie did not want to think about it. And she didn't want to talk about it either. She wanted to crawl under the blanket and hear nothing, see nothing and say nothing. She felt utterly overwhelmed. And torn like an old, discarded rag. As if someone had pushed her into a corner she couldn't escape from.

Up until now, she had delighted in the wonderfully effervescent feeling of being in love with Roman. It seemed so right, glorious, deep, romantic – and at the same time full of promise for an unlimited future together. Yet now, when it came down to it, she wasn't sure anymore. Was this really, truly what she wanted? To leave everything, her friends, her family, and start anew in a completely foreign place? Would she be able to do this?

She took the glass of Gin Tonic, that Maja had brought her, and automatically drank a large gulp. "Gee, you certainly mixed enough Gin into this…"

"That was necessary, sweetheart. I can see it and feel it: you are absolutely confused. But for Roman none of this is a game, on the contrary. I remember you saying often that this was all different and important and forever and so on. And now? The moment of truth has arrived, my friend.

"You know what, Natalie? Take a leap. Talk to your Papi. Better even: Sit down in silence for a couple of hours in the evening and try to hear your inner voice. Listen to what is going on within you. Just like Stefanos suggested. Perhaps it would also help to write down your thoughts and insights.

"How can you suddenly just not know anymore what you want? This surpasses even my imagination. My mother often said: 'Shit or get off the pot!' Which means: Make up your mind, darling. What in the name of the gods happened to your enormous love and adoration for Roman? You're not a little teenage ditz anymore, Natalie. Seventeen and a half, for Heaven's sake."

Maja was out of breath. She had worked herself into quite a state of exasperation. With a determined jerk of her head, she swung her raven hair backwards and stormed toward the window. She had had to learn very early in her life to stand on her own two legs. When she was thirteen, she competently took care of the whole household, brought home top grades from school and worked at the corner store in the evenings.

She was contemplating how differently Natalie had grown up: *Natalie was raised in a family that protected and guided her. She is intelligent and sometimes even courageous. And she has a great open heart with an enormous capacity for compassion.*

"Sorry darlin'! I didn't mean to blurt this all out the way I did. I suppose you are actually under shock. Take another sip, it will calm you down. And then, really, listen to your heart. What are you here for, Natalie? What is your calling? Your role in this life? What makes sense for you? You used to say you wanted to do something to end wars and poverty and pollution and injustice. Make love not war…

"I think Roman is right. In a country like Canada the two of you could achieve much more than here. So, you have another three weeks until you're going to Klosters. If this doesn't become clear to you by then, it will never be clear. And should this be the case, then so be it. I think it would be a shame, but not the end of the world. It would be the beginning of something else, something new. Cheers, my friend! I can't wait to hear the news!"

On her way home by tram through Basel, which was lit up festively with sparkling Christmas lights, Natalie felt as if a heavy rock, a mountain like the Matterhorn even, had been lifted from her shoulders. Maja was such an exceptional friend. Loyal. Lovely in every sense of the word. And even wise.

14

Natalie managed to find a moment to talk with Papi just before the holidays. It turned out that it hadn't really been necessary. Kurt Steiner understood his daughter perfectly. Had he been in Roman's shoes, he would have acted just the same. However, he wasn't willing to tell Natalie this. He also wouldn't speak about his great love he had left behind in California so many decades ago. Stefanos knew about it, of course. Kurt and Stefanos had been best friends then in Berkeley. The memories flooded Kurt like one of those enormous waves of the Pacific:

The University of Berkeley, UCB, had been a different university from its inception in 1868. Far ahead of its time, UCB opened the International House in 1930, where students from all over the world, men and women, from any ethnic background and of any colour (to the outrage of many) were able to matriculate. The slogan became legendary: *A power for peace through human understanding.*

Kurt from Switzerland and Stefanos, several years older than Kurt, from Greece – a meeting of two young men at the campus of UCB in 1946, which turned into a life-long friendship within a few hours. It was just after World War II, and hope for a better world ran high amongst the young generation. The students were filled with enthusiasm and soaring hopes as if the world stood before a grandiose turn toward sanity.

Kurt fell utterly in love with quiet Lola and her dark, springy, wild curls, while Stefanos lost his heart to the effervescent Audrey, who had a dazzling smile and wore her blonde hair short like a boy. The four of them spent many nights without sleep in Lola and Audrey's two bedroom apartment on La Loma Ave. With more than just melancholy, Kurt remembered those unforgettable nights spent in conversation – sometimes hilarious, sometimes profound – with drinking, dreaming and making love.

Kurt did not want to return to Switzerland. Nevertheless, his student visa ran out at the end of 1947 and there was no possibility for renewal. Together with

Stefanos he researched and disputed and reapplied – to no avail. He was not going to leave without Lola. That was completely out of the question. Lola, however, thought that it had been clear from the beginning that she would not ever want to leave the USA. She was going back to her family's home in New Orleans.

It took years until Kurt had adjusted to life in the city of Basel, to the mostly intolerant Swiss attitude of anything foreign or wild, and to the stiff-necked populace of old Basel. Stefanos had to leave his beloved Audrey in the USA as well, which was, of course, nothing but cold comfort for Kurt. Whenever he had a chance, Kurt would write to Stefanos, who was completely reliable to answer within a few weeks. Sometimes Kurt even found a way to visit Stefanos on his volcanic rock, as he called Nisyros.

Kurt had to admit to himself that the visit to Stefanos' island (as Natalie called Nisyros) with the whole family this summer had been an exceptional success. Stefanos and the girls appeared to be much on the same wavelength, and the old Greek became even more radiant in their company. In the mild, velvety blue evenings under the dome of starlight, Kurt and Stefanos often had ample time to reminisce about their shining years in California. Sometimes their conversations veered to the mystery of life itself, to the world as it had been and was now, to the forgotten, abandoned gods – and yes, to the perplexing questions about death.

Kurt's mind returned to Natalie and Roman. He would have loved to help them. Except that he knew without a doubt that this would be the surest way to an impossible crisis in his marriage to Denise. He was not going to risk that. Not because of his status as a respected and successful lawyer, but because he loved his wife despite all her arrogant and sometimes dispassionate ways. Denise grew up in a difficult, loveless home and began to blossom into a beautiful lady when she married Kurt. She was an intelligent and faithful companion, who knew how to prepare delicious meals and throw grand dinner parties. No, he was not going to risk his marriage, not even for his beloved daughter Natalie.

Kurt and Natalie were sitting in the living room of the old-fashioned yet comfortable and stylishly furnished house at St. Albanring in Basel. Kurt had relaxed in his large, dark brown and slightly worn leather armchair, a glass of Whisky on the rocks in his hand. Natalie was perched uneasily on the edge of the – in her eyes disgustingly ugly – olive-green sofa.

"But Papi, you said you understand me! But you don't give me any chance to live with Roman, to marry him, to build a life with him. He's no idiot, on the contrary. He is extremely smart in so many ways, he has common sense and he knows what he wants. And I love him."

"Natalie, I know. But try to think for a moment: You are only 17 and…"

Natalie had interrupted her father at the top of her voice: "I will be 18 next year!"

"Okay, you will be 18. Right. You have to first take your high school exam and then complete your studies at university to enable you to stand on your own two legs in your life. Whatever you would like to study, it will take years to achieve a degree. And in case you really don't want to go to university, you would have to commit to an apprenticeship of some kind or a college program, which will also take at least three years. So, tell me, how do you imagine this would work?"

"Why do you insist that I have to study something, Papi? I can learn many things without going to a college or university. I'm sure Roman can teach me a lot of useful skills himself."

The conversation bounced back and forth in this manner. There was no solution nor agreement in sight. After a seemingly endless hour, Natalie suddenly got up, ran to the door, opened it and then slammed it shut behind her. She was not be found anywhere. Kurt was not surprised, he had anticipated something like this. His heart was sore having had to disappoint his daughter in such a harsh way, as it felt to him now. As if he had abandoned her when she needed him most. *It's definitely not easy to choose between a daughter and a marriage...* he thought gloomily. He downed his drink and returned to his office upstairs.

Several decades later, shortly before Kurt died, he would speak with Natalie of that long-ago conversation. He would also tell her about California and Lola. And

about his marriage to Denise, which had been an enjoya-
ble and important partnership in his life, regardless of the
various obstacles. Father and daughter would hold each
other's hands, tears quietly running down both faces. To
Natalie it would feel as if they had truly found each other
again in mutual understanding.

But, of course, neither of them knew then, in December 1969, how the future would look.

15

December 25, 1969 was a Thursday. Since her talk with Papi, Natalie couldn't shake her dismay completely, but they were at Hotel Silvretta now and everyone's mood had rapidly turned mirthful. To celebrate Christmas even more festively, the Steiners had dinner at the Rôtisserie in the hotel. And to the surprise of them all, Roman was their waiter.

The main course was a deliciously tender roasted rack of lamb, accompanied by a luscious fig sauce and flavourful herbed potatoes. Something appeared to be stuck under Natalie's plate. It was a small piece of paper, a note from Roman: *Do you have time tomorrow after breakfast? In the lounge; I have to clean up; nobody there. RC*

Natalie found an excuse the next morning to leave for the lounge for a few minutes. Roman had left the door, which was usually locked at this time, open for her. He was already busy shining up the various glasses when

Natalie entered. She loved how the lounge smelled: old, cold cigarette smoke, timeworn leather, a hint of lemon and alcohol.

She stood motionless, entirely taken by Roman's appearance. He was wearing washed-out blue jeans and a thick, dark blue wool sweater. *I love him,* she realized, *there's not a hint of a doubt.* Still standing transfixed, she watched Roman as he put a strand of his thick, chestnut-coloured hair back in place with his left hand. He then smiled his breathtaking half smile, strode toward her and took her in his arms. Just like the first time, in the meadow by the Landquart, the kiss began slow and soft and lingering.

"Finally, my mountain faery, finally!" More kisses.

"Roman, I have to go skiing in a few minutes. As you know, Mama registered Margo and me as always in the ski school. It's just so unnecessary… Anyhow, we'll have to meet on an evening when you don't have to work late."

"Yes, sure, Natalie. Monday night. After your dinner. We'll say we'll go to the disco at the Casa Antica with the others. I'll wait outside. It's not very cold these days."

* * *

Eventually, the Silvretta crew was done with their work. Roman was sitting comfortably on his massive bed in room #1. He grabbed his tattered notebook and began:

Christmas 1969. It's almost midnight. Natalie is here! We can meet Monday, just she and I. It will all work out. All through the past years, I have had inherent trust in life itself, in the gods or the universe. To live without trust would be inconceivable for me.

Admittedly, I have fallen flat on my face more than once. But I got up again every time. And each time something went wrong, I learned something of value. Something that helped me to move forward in my little, unimportant, important life.

Natalie will be surprised at how my plans have evolved since I last wrote to her. My uncle in Alberta was quite convinced that there were no obstacles to hinder my immigration. And once we are married – voilà, needless to say, my wife will accompany me.

Hmm… what if Natalie won't say yes?? Because of her parents? Roman, stop it. Trust, remember?! TRUST!!

Yesterday I wrote a poem. For Natalie. In English.

The beloved

Broken open
so unexpectedly
silence speaking the unspoken

Tears of relief
I found you
As if I had lost you

And no, it's not you
it's not me either

It's the singing
of two tuning forks
in perfect harmony

The gods
directing the dream
You are the beloved

16

February 2022

Natalie opened her eyes – and closed them immediately. Everything was brilliantly, blindingly white.

I'm here, on the bench above Garfiun, she remembered with some confusion. *I must have been completely gone; living in my past. As if space and time were utterly bendable, malleable, or perhaps irrelevant. Or even nothing but an illusion, a non-reality invented by human beings. I can just hear Stefanos saying something like that…*

Her face was hot, but the rest of her body was beginning to shiver with cold. It was high time for her to move and make her way down to the small mountain restaurant at Alp Garfiun. Natalie still had her snowshoes buckled to her feet; she buttoned up her down jacket, pulled on her gloves, donned her sunglasses and stood up.

How can I feel already this stiff after having used snowshoes for only such a short while!? Sure, I'm almost 70 – yet I thought I was in decent shape...

Thankfully, snowshoeing downhill was wonderfully easy. By the time she arrived at Alp Garfiun, several guests were sitting outside in the sun on the wooden benches covered with sheepskins. Natalie had had her share of sunshine and winter air for the moment. She entered the cozy, warm restaurant.

Ah, the aromatic and familiar scent of alpine pine! And of the barley soup they called Bündner Gerstensuppe. That would be perfect for lunch. A glass of Malanser Pinot Noir to go with it. And after perhaps even a mug of mulled wine. A warm, cozy, comfortable feeling spread through Natalie's whole body. There was hardly anyone inside now. Long after she had finished eating the nourishing and delicious soup, she stayed where she was, savouring the mulled wine, feeling snug and dreamy. The memories that surfaced so easily were crystal clear.

* * *

On Monday evening, December 29, 1969, Natalie and Roman met at exactly 8:30 in front of the Silvretta. Margo, the young Rocco, Kenny and two girls, who were unknown to Natalie, were on their way to the Casa Antica. Roman and Natalie entered the hotel again by the back door.

Natalie had no idea how many stairs they had climbed until Roman finally stopped just below the attic in front of a door with a red sign. It said in white letters 'Zimmer 1', room number one.

"Is this really the number of your room, Roman?"

"No, no, not officially. But for me it is room number one, my room, so I had this sign made, for fun."

There it was again, that barely discernible, mischievous and wildly charming smile. Irresistible.

Roman had meant to talk to Natalie first. But that was now out of the question. After a long, soft and yet fiery kiss, he slowly opened the zipper in the back of Natalie's pants suit and helped her out of it. He quickly undressed himself and drew Natalie down on his big bed. *I have imagined this so many times*, he marveled, *and now it's real…"* He kissed her eyes and her mouth, her tender neck, her full breasts. Then he stopped, still caressing her arms, her hands. Gently he smoothed some of her escaped locks away from her forehead and asked in his sonorous voice with the charming dialect from the Grisons: " Do you have any doubts, my mountain faery?"

Natalie shook her head. She had none whatsoever anymore. Roman was so loving, so caring, so tender – she wanted nothing more than feel his body and take him into the welcoming dark core of her womanness. The bed was soft, the candle on the window sill flickered, and everything was exactly how it was supposed to be.

* * *

They held each other, caressing, kissing, without words for moments or eons, Natalie didn't know. In the sweetness of the afterglow of their first lovemaking the world appeared to be so beautiful and absolutely perfect. Life was worth living. There was hope – and the future shone with adventure, mystery and love.

Again, Natalie's wild, umber locks had escaped and Roman smoothed them away. "We need to talk, love. About us. About our plans. I have an uncle in Canada, who is helping me to immigrate. There shouldn't be any hurdles or problems, he said. And you, my mountain faery, you'll come with me as my wife. Well, I suppose we have to actually get married first…"

Roman got up, his muscular body glistening in the candle light. His striking, lean face, adorned with the fine moustache and the small Jesus beard, was serious. He knelt down by the bed in front of Natalie: "Do you want to marry me and begin a new life with me, Natalie?"

His eyes, my God, his eyes are fathomless, so honest and so full of love and hope – that look penetrates to the deepest part of my being. Natalie's heart was literally skipping a beat. She held both sides of his face with her hands, looked into his brown, gold-flecked eyes and said without any hesitation or confusion: "Yes."

17

New Year's Eve! This was the end of the famous, infamous, tumultuous year of 1969. In a few hours, the new year would begin. And a new life for Natalie and Roman.

The entire great banquet room at the Silvretta was decorated with glimmering garlands. White candles stood elegantly in silver candle holders on the tables dressed in starched white linen, already littered with New Years' Eve bombs, hats and tiaras, serpentine throws, noise makers of all kinds and balloons for later use. The extensive, excellent dinner was over, and in the background the lounge musicians kept playing their low-key repertoire.

Drumroll! There she was, the famous Josephine Baker. She sang her melodious songs wearing a glittering costume and thigh-high silver boots. Natalie wasn't truly interested and her mind drifted often. But she had to admit that for a lady over 60, the Black Venus was fantastic. 'J'ai deux Amours…'

Roman was around, of course, serving in his elegant black and white waiter's suit, complete with a black satin bow tie. Natalie was absorbed in this handsome love of hers and the memories of the tender and passionate night at his room, Zimmer 1. She tried to figure out, albeit without much enthusiasm, how to reveal her decision to her parents. It might be better to only talk to Papi…

Her thoughts were interrupted by Josephine Baker, who stood beside her, finishing one of her songs. She took Natalie's hand, turned it over and said quietly: "Your life will be an interesting adventure. Follow your dreams, always. More I cannot tell you…" Josephine disappeared between other tables, singing 'Paris, Paris, Paris'. Natalie was completely confused. What had this been all about?

Happy New Year! Bonne Année! Äs guats Nüüs!

Champagne corks popped and flew through the hall. The table bombs were lit and exploded, spilling more paper decorations and silly hats that were put on, the noise crackers went off noisily. The band in the background played Etta James now, Louis Armstrong and Frank

Sinatra. Music her parents enjoyed, but to Natalie this was annoyingly old-fashioned.

Roman had been watching Natalie. He had noticed that Josephine had taken her hand and had told her something. He wanted to know what it was, preferably right now. But, needless to say, he couldn't. The status quo had to be held upright at all cost. Only years later Natalie would share Josephine's words with him.

Roman was quite taken by how Natalie looked tonight. She was elegant in her dark blue dress, finely patterned in white, and her silvery nylons. She must have tamed her wild brunette hair so that it fell in shiny waves to her shoulders. And her makeup subtly enhanced the natural glow of her lovely face.

So, there it was, the new year. 1970. It would be the year of great change, the year of his new life. Roman was completely sure of this. His mind returned to their night together, wondering when he could touch her again. Perhaps he should just ask Papi for her hand in the old-fashioned way...

His reveries were interrupted by his fellow waiter and friend, Gino of the glowing charcoal eyes. "Come on, presto, presto, amico. Cosa sogni?"

* * *

Roman couldn't sleep. It was already 2:30 in the morning. He was lying on his bed, tired to the bone, but his mind wouldn't stop turning. He had to let Natalie know somehow that he was going to speak with her father. He knew there was a risk to that, that it could go wrong. Nevertheless, he saw no other option. He would also try to call his best friend Dumeng from a phone booth in the village early next morning.

Before sleep found him at long last, Roman read Hermann Hesse's poem 'Stufen'. He loved and admired Hesse's work. This poem had brought him solace in many a difficult moment:

*Stufen - Stages

As every flower fades and as all youth
Gives way to age, so life at every stage,
So every virtue, wisdom and all truth,
Blooms in its day and may not last forever.
As life may summon us at every age -
Be ready, heart, for parting, new endeavor,
Be ready bravely and without remorse
To find new brilliance old ties cannot give.
In all beginnings dwells a magic force
Protecting us and helping us to live.

Cheerfully let us move through different places
And let no sentiments of home detain us.
The Cosmic Spirit seeks not to restrain us
But lifts us stage by stage to wider spaces.
If we cling to comforts of our own making,
Familiar habits make for indolence.
We must prepare for parting and leave-taking
Or else remain the slave of permanence.

Even the hour of our death may send
Us youthful on to fresh new fields,
Life's call to us will never end
So be it, heart: bid farewell and heal.

Part Two – Canada

1

Roman's Swissair flight landed in Toronto, Canada on April 22, 1970 – the first Earth Day in the USA. What an auspicious beginning for a new life! One of the most famous Hippies of the 60s lead the celebrations in Philadelphia. These were the most peaceful demonstrations by millions of people in almost all cities of the country that the United States of America have ever experienced.

Pearson International Airport. *Large, but not pretty,* mused Roman upon arrival. No matter; he just had to pass through Immigration, he had all his papers, and then on to a flight to Edmonton with CP Air. His uncle would meet him there.

Roman was looking forward to a life in this enormous country, where there appeared to exist so many areas that civilsation hadn't touched. The expanse he saw looking out of his little window in the airplane was utterly unbelievable. He was equally anticipating to meet his uncle again, whom he had not seen since he was a child. Uncle Wally. Roman had to chuckle. When Wally was still living in Sent, he was called Walter.

Immigration and Customs had been no problem. Roman sat down on one of the uncomfortable seats, covered in hideous blue vinyl, by the departure gate. He was thinking of Natalie. And of the fact that everything had gone wrong, after all. At least for now.

Two days after New Year's Eve, Roman found an opportunity to speak with Kurt Steiner early one morning in the closed lounge. He had asked officially, and with all the man-to-man charm he could muster, for Natalie's hand in marriage. Although it was an outdated, old-school kind of move, Roman was sure, it would be the only strategy Dr. Steiner would even consider.

The smell of old, stale cigarette smoke in the lounge nauseated Roman on that Friday morning. It didn't help that Natalie's father held to his own point of view despite the fact that he was sincere in his understanding of Roman's plight.

"Roman, you know that I am quite fond of you. You also know that I love my daughter. I understand how the two of you feel much more than you can imagine. And I am thankful to you that you have the courage to speak with me honestly.

"It is too early – for both of you. Natalie has to finish her school and then begin her post-secondary education. I am convinced that it would be best for both of you if you first settled in Canada. Find your bearings, look for work, establish a home. Then we can all re-visit your proposal."

The conversation had neither been uncomfortable nor surprising. Nevertheless, Roman still felt as if someone had punched him in the stomach. In other words: He often felt miserable and sad, despite the excited anticipation about his adventures in Canada. Natalie would follow in time. This he knew with that unequivocal certainty that sometimes arises by the grace of the gods.

* * *

Just like Roman's flight from Zurich to Toronto, his flight to Edmonton was smooth and without incident.

"Hey there, young man!" That booming voice had to be Uncle Wally's. He was a large man with shoulders like a lumberjack. He wore an impressive cowboy hat, barely containing his thick, greyish mane, and brown leather boots. A blue-black-white checkered shirt, slightly stretched over Wally's midsection, blue jeans, a leather belt with a massive silver buckle in the shape of a bull's head completed the picture. His tanned, clean-shaven face broadened into a hearty smile.

Roman felt like a little boy in Wally's bear-like embrace. His luggage, an oversized red backpack, arrived promptly, and the two men left the airport within minutes. Outside it was more than just cold. An icy wind blew from the North, and Romans' hands were quickly getting stiff. *Canada's reputation for freezing temperatures is definitely not exaggerated,* the Swiss mountain lad mused.

Soon they were bouncing northwest with Wally's dark blue pickup truck, a rattly, big, old GMC. Outside of the city, the fields were still frozen and Roman saw patches of lingering snow. Alberta's North was immense and rough, wilderness and forests mixed with extensive farms. Far to the West, in a bluish haze, Roman was able to discern the white peaks of the Rocky Mountains.

The truck smelled of old vinyl and diesel. The radio was blaring country music non-stop. Roman felt as if he had time-travelled back to at least 30 years ago. There was a tangible shift, it seemed to him, as if life proceeded on another level, closer to nature and farther from civilization. Or perhaps it was just that civilization here was so much younger that it appeared to be still in close connection with the land, the climate and the changing of the seasons.

The old GMC rattled and puffed along highway 43. Wally mentioned that they needed at least eight to nine hours for the 500 km to Beaverlodge, if not more. Other than that, Roman's uncle was mostly silent or he sang heartily along with the country songs. Roman was completely at ease with that. It gave him the opportunity to sink into the wide landscape that changed from grey, brown or white fields to dark green forests the more northward they drove. He was fascinated by the size of the farms with their rusty-red painted homes and barns – there was no comparison to the tiny Swiss alpine farm-steads. What impressed and astonished him the most, though, was the utter sense of endlessness of this coun-try.

Would Natalie feel the same way?

2

February 2022

It was February 16, and Natalie was still sitting on the
wooden bench in the warm, cozy restaurant at Alp Garfiun. She remembered how she had written to Stefanos
immediately after Roman had left for Canada. She also
remembered his reply, which she had stuffed into her
daypack on impulse before leaving the hotel. She felt like
reading it again now, a few stains, frayed edges on the
once lovely handmade paper and a bit of smeared ink
notwithstanding:

May 1970

Agapiméni mou!

*My sincere and heartfelt thanks to you, dear Na-
talie, for your trust and your friendship. As I wrote
in my previous letter, I am deeply honoured.*

Roman is in Canada, now. A separation like this is never easy for a young love and young people. I am taking the risk of sounding like an old codger spouting an old cliché: Such is life. Indeed, Natalie. Life never ceases to present us with new challenges – we can either grow with or through them, or we can ignore them. Every obstacle is an opportunity. Every rock lying in your path is a chance.

An old master told me once upon a time that the most important task for a person is to pursue the development of what we call the self in order to become a true human being. Without that, we are not only lost as a human being, we are also useless. When we find clarity with and within ourselves, then we can bring a lot of good to the world. We can lighten the energies on this beautiful planet Earth we call home and we can genuinely help other beings.

Life asks us for the willingness to face challenges, so that we may harvest the fruits of the thorn-bushes of difficult situations and phases. There is a great need to stop to be able to hear the small, soft voice of the soul. In the buzz of everyday modern life this faint whisper is often completely lost. It can be truly helpful to sit in silence by a tree, a river, a beach or a meadow, away from buildings and people. This is how we may learn to really see and hear.

Of course, this is not an easy thing to do for a young, vivacious lady like you. I understand that. But life is never easy – and it is not meant to be. If you would try to spend a bit of your time quietly in nature, dear Natalie, you may find answers you did not expect. Write to me about the revelations and insights you encountered.

Remember: You are always in my heart.
Is to epanidín! Until we meet again!

Stefanos

PS: Consider that Roman has to find his own way first in the far country of Canada before you can follow him there.

* * *

When Stefanos reread the letter he had just written, he was not sure whether Natalie would understand what he was trying to say. Whether he himself had even interpreted the thoughts and enquiries of a young person correctly or whether he was biased by the decades of experiences of his own life.

He got up from his hard wooden chair, fetched a cigarillo and a glass of the slightly tart Greek red wine he so enjoyed, and left the house through the narrow back door. The veranda was all but hidden by the abundant growth of numerous brilliantly pink Bougainvillea. It was one of those azure blue evenings when the neighbouring islands seemed to float mysteriously in the mists over the southern Aegean Sea.

Stefanos was dressed in his usual summer attire: bleached-out Khaki shorts and a white cotton button down shirt, both intensifying his dark brown skin, his sea-blue eyes and his thick, silver-grey short hair. He sat down on one of the two wicker chairs, crossed his still muscular legs and took a deep draw of his cigarillo.

Roman and Natalie – they remind me so much of Natalie's father and his Lola, he thought. *Those were the days back then in Berkeley! And nothing, nothing at all, has changed in Kurt's life. The only inner voice he followed was with regards to his profession.*

We were post-war children – actually doubly so: born after the First World War, we experienced the second as young men. We wanted nothing but peace and love and freedom. And it seemed just as possible back then in Berkeley in 1946 as it did in Woodstock in 1969. The Hippie movement is almost absurdly similar in many ways to the dreams and hopes we had.

And yet, it seems to me, everything continues as before: Kurt has made a career, married an extremely

*beautiful woman whom he appreciates but does not love;
and the world continues to turn in its war-infatuated and -
infested power as it did at the beginning of this century –
and as it actually had in all the past thousands of years.
The Vietnam War – a monstrosity. . .*

*Can I do justice to Natalie and Roman with my experi-
ences and insights? A new love – and still, life just takes
its usual course. There are moments when I can see into
the heart of my old friend Kurt, and I realize why he
couldn't agree to the marriage right now. In his many
years as a lawyer, Kurt had to accept and subscribe to a
lot of rules, regulations and social conventions. Still, I
would have expected a little more understanding from
him, especially with regard to his Lola back then. His
sweet little Lola. . .*

Stefanos had gotten lost in his thoughts; he emptied
his wine glass and pulled himself together:

*The two young lovers have to get through this. Life in
this world can so often be hard, unpredictable and unjust.
Everything depends on inner stability, how to overcome*

the hurdles. And I sincerely hope that I can be a support to Natalie. So that she can also recognize the wonders and the deep, real joy of life amidst the challenges.

3

2022

Natalie was ready to leave the Alp Garfiun. Today she would certainly not walk to the Stone Circle, and probably not for a few days. It was February 16 – she had a good week left. Although today the moon would be full – just like when she first met with Roman in July 1969. It seemed so long ago.

Back in her hotel room she enjoyed the spicy scent of pinewood and indulged herself in a spruce needle bath. Then she slipped under the warm blanket and opened another notebook by Roman. She was thinking of calling Maja afterwards.

> *10 May 1970*
> *Now I've been here for two and a half weeks at Uncle Wally's buffalo farm. Absolutely extraordinary, this wide, wild landscape. And the buffaloes, the bison – truly ancient creatures full of strength*

and herd instinct. Wally is a great person, gener-
ous and open, and he has a big heart for everyone: for people, for animals, for nature, for life.

My soul can breathe, open up, blossom. People who live here don't just live "on" the land, they
live with the land, with nature. And that's exactly
what urban populations and overcivilized people
have lost: the connection to what life actually
means. That's why I'm here. That's why I have to
convince Natalie as soon as possible that this really is our common path – the only path.

For now, however, my journey takes me even
further north! Wally got me a job in the Yukon Territory! With an 'outfitter', who leads tourists with
horses into the mountains to hunt. He's got to be
a quirky guy. His name is Sean McArthur. The
company is not very big, but I'm sure that I can
gain a wealth of experience there for a life in the
Canadian wilderness.

Recently, I read something by Rumi that I liked. I'll quote it here, but not completely verbatim:

The universe is not outside of you.
Look inside yourself;
everything that you want – you are already that.

Yes, that is exactly the way it is. Next time I write to Natalie, I'll send her these lines. I think it's important that she understands that. Her uncle Stefanos must be someone who thinks like that. I've often wondered if I should just write to him...

Our address in Canada – I can already see it in front of me:

'Natalie and Roman Camenisch
Sundown Farm, Alberta'

Or something like that...

Natalie put the notebook aside. She was reminiscing about the full life she had lived. The work in the retirement homes and animal welfare had been interesting and rewarding – and fulfilling her need to be useful or beneficial to others. She loved her friends, especially Maja, and Margo, her sister. Still, it hurt.

"Maja, it's so good to hear your voice!"

"It's about time, old gal!" – that was a typical Maja response. "Well, how is life in beautiful, illustrious Klosters? Have you met any celebrities? Have you been snowshoeing yet?"

"Snowshoeing, yes. Celebrities, no. The new Silvretta is great. Now called Silvretta Parkhotel Klosters. Of course… no longer 'my' Silvretta, but extremely pleasant, tasteful, lots of pinewood, great cuisine, and the owner is a competent, extremely friendly host. Christian Erpenbeck. Just as amiable as Giorgio Rocco was then, but completely different. Christian is tall and very slim, about 50, I think. His face is soft and striking at the same time, and in his bright eyes I think I see a little melancholy. Be that as it may, he's always open to conversation. That's great.

"Anyway... Imagine – I finally dared to look into Roman's notebooks! There's a lot coming up..." Natalie paused to support her back with a second pillow.

"I'd like to read a bit to you, Maja, if you like."

"Absolutely! I'd love that."

"Well, this entry – like many others, in black ink; these beige-grey notebooks look like they have yellowed, but I don't think so – that's just the way they look... – Well, this entry is from June 12, 1970 – my birthday...

Friday, 12 June 1970

Natalie's birthday. She's 18 now! I wrote to her, but I don't know if she'll get the letter with the dried flowers in time. According to Sean, Canada Post is not always reliable.

It's unbelievable, this life here in the wild. Everything I could ever dream of. As if we were already so far removed from nature, from life (!) in the 'civilized world' that we can no longer imagine what it

*means to live with the rhythm of nature – of life. I
already knew that, I think. But now that I am here,
amidst the vastness, the woods, the mountains
(without the cable cars!), the peace and solitude;
where bears live and wolves, moose, lynx and
many other animals in abundance – only now do I
feel deeply how alienated we are from life. Actually,
it's a tragedy...*

*Here, in the farthest corner of the McClintock Val-
ley, a good 50 kilometers from Whitehorse, life still
breathes in its original rhythm. Sean and I get water from the spring with big containers. If we want
hot water, it must be heated on the wood stove.
This means that wood has to be split and brought
to the log house.*

*There is no electricity. Light is not a big thing in
summer, since we are already very far north here.
On rainy days we use candles and oil lamps, as we
do in winter. Vegetables are available from the 'root
cellar' (it's still too early for the garden), meat we
have plenty from hunting on Sean's land, bread*

and eggs we get from the neighbour. The horses have to be fed with last year's hay and oats, as the grass is still very sparse.

In the evenings we often sit by the fire under the incredibly huge sky that doesn't really get dark. Yet we see thousands of stars. The Northern Lights won't be visible until autumn because it is so bright at night. We hear the owls, sometimes a wolf or several, a crack in the woods. We treat ourselves to a sip (or several) of Canadian Rye Whisky, maybe even a cigar.

Sean sometimes tells one of his stories. He's about 50 years old, muscular, medium-sized, his eyes are of an unusually bright blue, his beard is dense and, like his lush hair, blond-gray-brown: grizzly colours. There are plenty of them around here, the grizzlies. I am not afraid, but I have great respect for them – and all wildlife. A full-grown male grizzly is an impressive sight with a good 400 kg and about 2½ meters tall when standing on his *hind legs. As a human being, I actually feel small and powerless.*

Sean has been living here alone for a few years. Not only does he run a small tourist business, he is also a trapper and hunter, horse owner and lumberjack. His face is always tanned, his eyes sparkle with a boyish kind of mischief, and I don't think he has anything else in clothes than jeans, shirts and jackets made of denim. As with Wally, this includes a leather belt with metal buckle and a broad brimmed hat.

Sean's stories are something special. I was going to write one down here and send it to Natalie, but now I'm too tired. Tomorrow morning, we'll leave again at 5 o'clock. The self-made wooden beds have skins and wool blankets – much better than mattresses and down duvets. And there is no electricity and its buzz...

I no longer wonder what could be better. The only thing missing is Natalie.

4

February 2022

"So cool, Natalie!" Maja thought that even after all these years, it was not easy for both her and Natalie to talk about Roman. Especially now that Natalie managed to read his innermost thoughts for the first time and might be able to understand him.

"We had such great dreams, Maja. After the two world wars and especially with the Vietnam War, so to speak, in our bones – and although that war was far away from us, it was our generation that grew up with it. For Roman and me, there was only one thing: to live in peace, equality, nature-awareness and mindfulness, and perhaps even to pass it all on to others. That's what we would have done. In Canada..."

Natalie tried not to cry the tears that were burning behind her eyes. For decades, she had forbidden herself to think such thoughts. She had chosen, in the spirit of

Roman's commitment to peace and authenticity, a tranquil life in which she supported people, animals and nature in her own way. In the past decades, she had worked or helped in animal shelters, nursing homes and retirement homes, and had taken the lead in countless nature conservation initiatives. She had a big heart and never said no when someone truly needed her.

But she had not managed to travel to Canada and realize Roman's idea of a permaculture farm and school. Yes, permaculture: the creation of one's own stable and sustainable ecosystem, in which the responsible use of water, planting, animal husbandry, co-existence with insects and wildlife is modelled on the natural course of nature – this would have been the design of their way of life. And, if possible, in combination with other like-minded people, who also trusted in the interaction and interconnectedness of all aspects of humanity, nature and the universe.

Natalie often thought of the Findhorn Foundation in Scotland, which started very small and almost involuntarily in 1962 and was already organized as an official community ten years later. Over the decades, the community had grown to over 400 members. There was everything – from permaculture to a spiritual way of life, from peaceful coexistence and work to workshops and seminars. Many times, Natalie wanted to make a trip to the Northeast of Scotland; she never did. And this year, Klosters was more important.

"Are you still there, Natalie?"

"Sorry, Maja, just had a few thoughts that came up. – So, anyway, what do you think about this entry by Roman?"

"So amazing how he was able to draw closer to himself in this life in the wilderness. And how you were always in his thoughts and in his plans. What an extraordinary young man... By the way, do you have anything else you would like to read to me?"

"I only looked into a few notebooks, Maja. He wrote at least six a year... Well, here's one that I haven't opened yet. I'll just read it to you... - it starts exactly three years after he emigrated, here's an excerpt from June, again:"

June 12, 1973

My beloved mountain faery is now 21! It's hard to believe.

I'm sitting here on my fur-covered wooden bed in Sean's log cabin in McClintock Valley, three candles light up my small room, and I'm just realizing that I always live in small rooms: at home in Sent, and then at the Silvretta in Klosters, and even at Wally's Farm – is there a meaning behind it? Anyway, today Sean brought me two letters: one from Natalie and one from Stefanos. What a surprise!

"What!? I had no idea Roman was in contact with Stefanos, Maja! Neither Roman nor Stefanos ever talked about it. Unbelievable... So, next:"

"Wait a minute, Natalie. Roman asks himself if there is a meaning behind his small rooms, I would say that as a person/soul he had such greatness that he didn't need any spatially."

«What an eloquent thought, Maja; Roman would beam his mischievous half-smile if he heard you. Maybe he does... Still, let's carry on now:"

So, I had the joy of deciding which letter to read first. And if you, dear Natalie, should ever go through these notes, forgive me for reading Stefanos' message first. Instead of writing about it, the original is in the appendix. What a man, that Stefanos! I would almost like to equate him with Socrates.

"Natalie, look what Stefanos had written!"

Natalie had gone to the ornate pine table in order to be able to sit better than in bed. She retrieved Stefanos' letter – the beloved handwriting of her favourite uncle on the always same handmade stationery:

In May 1973

File mou
I thank you from the bottom of my heart for your

*lines and your confidence, Roman. There is a lot
of poetry and depth in your words. Natalie made
the perfect choice.*

*Life demands a lot of us. As you write, there are
moments when your path seems to be full of
stones and abysses. I understand. Financing your
own farm is a big investment, and you're not the
man to beg for money. Natalie's father would
have the resources, but neither you nor Natalie
are willing to ask Kurt. I understand that, too.*

*Could you imagine buying a piece of property in
another province where it would be cheaper to
buy land? Even without existing buildings? I'm
sure you'd have enough savings for that. I also
firmly believe that Natalie will come to you as
soon as possible. Together with your friends, you
will manage to make a start. Every step is part of
the journey.*

Goethe said:
Whatever you can do, or dream of doing, begin it!

Courage has genius, power and magic in it.

And Hesse:

> In all beginnings dwells a magic force
> protecting us and helping us to live.

You see, file mou, these two great men knew this, as so many before them. We have to take the step, the beginning – and then the sources of the universe open up and the latent possibilities flow. I know you understand. I also know that's how you live your life. Otherwise, you wouldn't have had the courage to ask for Natalie's hand or to venture to Canada. So, I'm not worried that you don't have the strength for your path in yourself. Keep going!

Life is a miracle, Roman. It is our obligation and duty to live it with all our soul, with an open heart and mind, with joy, enthusiasm, passion, gratitude and courage.

May the grace of the gods and the light of the stars accompany your and Natalie's path.

Stefanos

PS: I look forward to your next letter!

5

"Wow, Natalie! And you had no idea that the two were corresponding. Fantastic!"

Natalie tried to figure out what she felt. Not jealousy, no, not at all. But perhaps a small, aching sadness that neither her great love Roman nor her beloved Uncle Stefanos had ever told her that they were in contact with each other. But she also felt a deep, warm joy: the two had found the way to each other.

"Yes, Maja, that really amazes me. It's actually like this: we are unable to truly look into another person's soul. We can only see what the other person is willing to show us. Even Stefanos... I have to assume that Roman had asked him not to tell me about it. And the fact that Stefanos had kept that promise until his death – this, of course, testifies to his deep integrity and wisdom. Yes, that's how I can fully understand and accept it."

Meanwhile it was dark outside, but the full moon would soon rise over the white peaks and bathe the valley and the mountains in its silver light. Natalie loved the moonlight as Roman had loved it. She found moonlight to be gentle and calming, peaceful and also mysterious. 'By the power of the moon' many things had already happened in this world...

"So, let me read on in Roman's entry from June 1973. Maybe there are more surprises, Maja....:"

Of course, Stefanos – now I actually wanted to write Socrates... – is right: I have to take the first step. I've probably been in this beautiful wilderness of the Yukon far too long without really caring about opportunities elsewhere. The Yukon is great with its solitude and vastness; Alberta and British Columbia are also breathtakingly beautiful. But the prices of the farms or even just the land are too high. Maybe I'll talk to Sean sometime.

To be honest, and this is what I definitely want to be here in my notes: Stefanos' letter

touched me very much. The fact that he an-
swered me is not only a small miracle for me, but
also a proof of his kind wisdom. I wish there were
many more such people. Thank you, Natalie, for
my meeting your uncle through correspondence —
although you do not know that.

Tomorrow, we'll go to the mountains with
the horses. I am happy every time we return to
the 'backcountry'. There is still snow up there, but
it's high time to prepare the two cabins for the
guests. Brégo (after Aragorn's horse in Tolkien's
'The Lord of the Rings'!), my big, strong horse,
has the sunny colours of a Haflinger. He's a super
friendly gelding, and I don't know how I would be
able to just leave without him when the time
comes...

The world of JRR Tolkien, by the way, was
introduced to me through Sean. It seems to me
that in the US and Canada most people who like
to bury themselves in a book have read 'The Lord
of the Rings'. I can't believe what this man has

accomplished. A whole mythology, cosmology in-
cluding the origin of the world, thousands of years
of history, several completely new languages and
fantastic peoples. Unique. I hope Natalie has al-
ready received her first book, 'The Fellowship of
the Ring'. And I hope she'll be as excited as I am.

Now, I'll have one more sip of Rye and then
I'll go to bed and read Natalie's letter. It's a lovely
thing to do before falling asleep.

Oh, and before I forget: I've been looking
through a Greek-English dictionary (belongs to
Sean) because Stefanos is Greek. There I found
a word that describes him (according to Natalie) –
as well as his deep, calm wisdom: kefi.

"kefi - the spirit of joy, enthusiasm, high spir-
its and frenzy, in which good times and passion
for life are expressed with an abundance of ex-
citement, happiness and fun."
Good night.

* * *

Natalie had a smile on her lips when she finished reading. Yes, kefi was the perfect description for Stefanos.
And Roman – he too was enthusiastic, with heart and
soul in everything he did. Did the two of them ever meet?

"What do you think, Maja, could it be possible that Roman and Stefanos once met?"

"Now first of all, Natalie, kudos to both of them. I still
feel privileged to have met Stefanos on Nisyros in 1969.
My Goddess, that was ages ago!

"To answer your question, my gut tells me yes. And
when my inner voice says yes so immediately and
clearly, then I trust it. Why are you asking?"

"Because I always wanted them to get to know each
other. Maybe there's something about it in Roman's other
notes. You know, Maja, if that were really so – how wonderful! Even though I didn't know anything about it – what
a gift for these two. Stefanos would have liked to have a
son... But I know this only through Papi.

"So, here we go. I need to read on... not on the phone now, but in the next few days. Thanks for listening, agapiméni mou!"

"My pleasure, girlfriend! Change of subject: What is going to happen in the next few days with Klosters' 800th anniversary celebrations? I could come visit you for two or three days. Not at the Silvretta, it's too expensive for me. But they still have room at the Chesa Selfranga."

"Aha! You've already asked. That would be great, Maja! Then we can browse through Roman's notebooks together. Today is February 16th, I'm going to stay here until the 26th. On the 18th is the demo show of the ski schools; on the 25th and 26th Winterläbä with a snow show on Selfranga on the 25th; on the 26th the children's sleigh ride, that's a very old custom, and then the Gögel race – those are sleds – on Selfranga. Then you would be at the ideal place in the Chesa Selfranga."

"Exactly! I'll see you on the 21st – that's in five days. Promise me that you won't finish reading all of Roman's notes before I arrive. I'm so looking forward to being there with you, Natalie. By the way, Kris, Benno and Margo are sending greetings and love."

"I can't wait to see you, Maja. We haven't done anything together for far too long. Thanks for the greetings, and give them my love, too. See you soon and good night!"

"Nighty night, girlfriend!"

6

Natalie was more than tired from snowshoeing and the fresh mountain air. But also because of the emotions that all those memories had brought forth. She felt as if she had been carried away by a mountain stream, foaming over rocks and around many bends down the valley. She could not and did not want to sleep.

After the bath and the phone call with Maja, she freshened up, put on her favourite dress made of azure merino wool and went to the Stübli restaurant for a late dinner: a tender lamb entrecôte with nut crust, zucchini and red peppers and fried polenta corners. It was delicious. As always, Christian welcomed her with his charming smile.

She had returned to her room facing the park and snuggled into the wonderfully warm blanket on her bed, two pillows under her head.

How absolutely tremendous that Roman and Stefanos have found each other, she thought. *I want to know all about it. I'm sure Roman wrote more with regard to that somewhere. Maybe in one of the last notebooks.*

Natalie's instincts were on the button: Notebook # 29. This time written in pencil. She was now wide awake and ready to spend some time with Roman in a part of his past that she knew only partially. A shiver ran through her whole being with the thrill of reading more about the life of her great love.

* * *

1 June 1975
It's a Sunday. And I can't believe it: I'm on Nisy-ros!!! It was quite a trip... I haven't written for days. Oh, how absolutely grand to be here with Stefanos! My soul seems to float above the ultra-marine of the Aegean Sea like a transparent, weightless cloud.

Before I dive into the radiant Now and To-day, and although I have already written down tons of notes and thoughts about my life in the last two years, I want to do a small «backtrack» and venture a kind of summary:

In June 1973, I was still with Sean in the Yukon and was about to ride into the mountains. That's when I received Stefanos' first letter. From that point on, my own attitude to my life changed – or rather, how I handled my life. It's almost creepy how I can trace it back to that specific moment. Even today, two years later, the memory is crystal clear and unambiguous.

Sean had introduced me to Lester Ryan after the summer season, who, in addition to his 100 acres and farmhouse, owned a small, wild, undeveloped, inexpensive property a few miles down the valley. The Yukon is rough and the winters are hard and long. I had first-hand experience by now. But with perseverance and work and greenhouses, etc. – and with the long, bright summer days – growing vegetables and keeping animals is absolutely possible. Sean breeds animals, and Lester also keeps horses and cows. I bought the property on the spot! Natalie was a bit surprised – but she is an extraordinary woman with admirable openness and acceptance...

So, in the summer of '73 and '74 I was still in the mountains with Sean, the horses and the tourists. From late autumn to spring I was busy building a small cabin on my property. On my (our) property!! – The Yukon winter is, of course, not the time of year to build a cottage. If it hadn't been for Sean and Lester, I would not have had the courage to do it. Lester is a bear of a man, loud and good-natured, with a cheerful, round face. And his slim, warm wife Silvia is an excellent cook.

May 75. The farewell of Brégo was the worst. Although I know Sean will take loving care of my horse until I return, I cried every night on my trip south on the Alaska Highway. The term

"Highway" is an extreme exaggeration: it's a gravel road with countless bends and steeply sloping sections. I was hitchhiking and camping (not that I told Natalie exactly that) and would have had time to write while waiting for a ride, but my heart was so sore, I couldn't. I couldn't write to Natalie either. She forgave me later. Thank you, thank you, my mountain faery.

The one guy who picked me up at Rancheria in an old Ford trash box – his name was Charlie and he looked like a crook from an old Western – wanted to stop at the Liard Hot Springs. Liard is located about 200 km south of Watson Lake and already in BC. Fantastic! Natural hot water pools amidst lush greenery – and above them, from the steam of the sulphur springs after a night of heavy frost, ice crystals on all branches of trees and bushes. It looked like Dr. Zhivago's ice palace!

Then Muncho Lake, Fort Nelson, Pink Mountain and Fort St John. Charlie lived nearby, so my ride was over. Actually, it wouldn't have been too far from Beaverlodge, where Wally's farm is located. But I wanted to get to Vancouver as soon as possible to catch a flight to Toronto and on to Greece.

There was such turmoil in my soul and my heart was bleeding: Farewell to Brégo, to Sean and Lester, to the Yukon, to my lifestyle of the last 5 years!! And then the wild joy of meeting Stefanos and seeing Natalie again afterwards. I felt helplessly thrown back and forth like in a storm-whipped ocean.

Another poem by Maja Rim comes to mind... By the way, I finally found out that Natalie's friend Maja is actually Maja Rim! The world is a carousel, and we go round in circles....

Broken Open

I want to live
with a heart broken
open

so that I may feel
the suffering and the pain
of all beings

I want to allow
the heart to fall
apart
so that I may feel
compassion
for all beings

I want to feel
the tenderness of the heart
deeply
so that I may know
your sorrow and
mine

I want to know
the intimacy of the heart
even if it brings me
to my knees -
so I may live
fully

7

And so, I arrived on the island of Kos on May 31, 1975, with my big red backpack, an open heart and a lot of enthusiasm. Sweet, yet tart the Greek wine, blue-golden the night, spicy the smell of garlic and souvlaki. From the beach cafés, the melancholic sounds of the typical Dimotiki Mousiki floated through the alleys – what a different world!

From the picture book country of Switzerland to the wild North of Canada and now to the sun-scorched Aegean. The gods are playing their cards, and I'm in. It is almost awe what I feel: awe of the mystery of life. I'm sure Stefanos will have a lot to say about this...

I slept on the beach that summer night on Kos; the sparkle of the stars was my blanket and the rhythm of the waves my lullaby.

The next morning (yesterday) a ferry left for Nisyros, the small volcanic island, home of

Stefanos and countless goats. I was over-tired, over-wrought and terribly excited about this new adventure of my life. Questions and joy bubbled in my soul – or in other words: there were fireworks inside of me with glittering stars and shimmering question marks.

The ferry crossing - that was fantastic! The Aegean Sea showed its power with foaming waves that threw our wooden boat up and down like the proverbial nut shell. The captain – a small but imposing, darkly tanned, wordless man with scruffy grey hair, which was somewhat kept under control by a navy blue captain's cap – was calmness itself. The wind whipped my now more than shoulder-length hair, the sun glared at the wild sea and the salt water splashed high over the ship. Magnificent! Until that moment, I had not known that I loved this – as if I had always been at home in this element.

Mandraki, the capital of Nisyros. From afar I was impressed by the bright white monastery, which seemed to have grown out of the rock high above the city. Stefanos later told me its name: Panaghia Spiliani. The square houses of the city in their limestone white dress, some with sky-blue painted doors and window frames, awaited me like a prodigal son. I, a thorough Bündner Bergler, a mountain boy from the Grisons Alps, felt deeply moved by a feeling of coming home. Unbelievable.

Stefanos was waiting for me at the pier. I recognized him immediately: medium-sized, wiry, sunburned, white cotton shirt and shorts, thick grey hair and moustache – and a sparkling smile in his beautiful, wrinkled face. And the eyes! Intensely blue – cornflower blue maybe, deep and kind. Here again the crazy feeling of coming home. It was like I had known Stefanos forever before we even spoke a word. Uncanny...

"Kalosórises, fíle mou! Welcome, my friend!"

I knew that deep voice with the rolling `r`. For a split second, all the contours around me blurred, and I only saw the azure eyes and a silver star above them. I had goose bumps. Natalie is never going to believe this.

Stefanos gazed at me with a deep, knowing look and said softly:
"I know, Roman. I'll explain it to you. But first come, let's drive to my house. It's only about 13 kilometers to Nikia, but the road winds up to an altitude of about 400 meters above the Aegean Sea. With my old rattle box, it takes at least half an hour. Besides, we always expect goats on the road."

A wink - and there it was – the laughter Natalie had told me about: resounding, raucous and full of gaiety.

Nikia, high up on the mountain, white-blue houses. The village was nestled gradually between rocks in a daring, dangerous and often

precarious way. The streets were paved with
stones and so narrow that hardly two people
could walk side by side. Amazing. And then Stefa-
nos' house, as Natalie had described it: white, of
course, with blue doors and window frames, the
garden overgrown with dark pink bougainvillea,
and the breathtaking view over the steep slopes
to the azure sea. Magical.

The gods be great thanks for this unique life
I've been given.

8

2022

That's where the notebook ended. Natalie had a hard time returning from the worlds of Nisyros, Stefanos and Roman. She had to make sure she was still in the warm bed in room 408 at the Silvretta Parkhotel in Klosters. It was February 16, 2022 - not May/June 1975... She looked at her clock on the bedside table: it was almost midnight. Natalie got up, opened the balcony door and breathed in the fresh, cold snow and mountain air. The full moon illuminated the white of the mountains with gleaming silver light, and she was pretty sure she saw Castor and Pollux, the two brightly shining stars in the sign of Gemini.

One feels so small and insignificant at the sight of these radiant natural phenomena..., she thought. *An experience of humility and relief, even bliss. We're not so terribly important, given the size and incomprehensibility*

*of the universe. Stefanos has contributed a lot to the way
I feel and understand this in a deeper sense today.*

The next morning greeted Natalie with sunshine and a knock on the door. It was the little blond waiter who brought her fresh Gipfeli (croissants), milk coffee, various jams, fruit salad and a smile. Today she indulged herself in the luxury of breakfast in bed.

Natalie wanted to talk to Maja again. But not today. *I should call Margo, too,* she thought. *Ever since she has been together with Benno, she has really blossomed. It's a pity Mama and Papi did not live to see it.*

Three fulfilled, sunny snow days later she called Maja: "Guten Morgen, liebe Sorgen, seid ihr auch schon alle da?" Which meant something like: "Good morning, dear sorrows, are you all here already?"

"Well, good morning to you, sweetness! What gives me the honour of your call? Everything ok, Natalie?"

"Yes, of course, Maja – but there is something I wanted to tell you... Do you have time?"

"Sure. Always for you. I'll just get my coffee." Maja wore her beloved blue-turquoise kimono over the leggings and undershirt made of merino wool. She loved the feeling of cuddly warmth.

"Well, you can start now, Natalie. I'm sitting on my sofa, warmly wrapped in my blanket that I had brought – so many years ago... – from Kashmir."

"I am so looking forward to seeing you here in Klosters, Maja! The demo show of the ski school two days ago – in the evening, of course – was fantastic, really. I used to ski for decades, but what was offered here in terms of skills, acrobatics and snow dancing – that was phenomenal! Too bad you missed that.

"But that's not why I'm calling. I don't think I ever told you that Philip Günthardt – you remember, he was a member of our Klagemauer group at the time – became my doctor. Cardiology is his specialty... I would never have imagined him becoming a physician. Remember, he was such a long, gangly youth with his wild, blond curls and freckles, and he always had a joke on his lips and a wink in his water-blue eyes. Anyway...

"Well, I recently went for a routine check-up like every year; and also because I had the feeling that my heart seemed to be beating a little irregular at times. Philip did the usual tests – and the results showed nothing out of the ordinary. Of course, he advised me not to overwork myself, not to stress myself, etc. You know me, agapi-méni mou – there has been very little stress in my life for years. I just wanted to tell you."

Natalie did not tell Maja, however, that while snow-shoeing she had had the feeling that her heart started to beat quite hard sometimes and that she had been a bit short of breath.

"Why didn't you ever talk about it, Natalie? We're life friends! We always talk about everything, whether it's joy-ful or sad or difficult."

"Of course, Maja, thankfully! But it's all right, and I don't like to talk about my boo-boos – everyone else does it all the time. I find such conversations utterly unin-spiring and tasteless."

"And now you're almost 70, girlfriend, and healthy! Anyway, thank you for your confidence. I'm glad you opened your heart to me in this respect, too. By the way, I'll be with you in two days. Then I'll be able to take care of you!"

Maja's warm laughter released the tension. *Stefanos used to remind me that I could and should talk to Maja about everything,* Natalie remembered. How she would love to be with him now on his small veranda, high above the Aegean Sea. His simple and deep wisdom had always been a great comfort to her. But alas: Tempi passati.

9

1975

Stefanos and Roman sat on that very veranda on the evening of a sunny day in June 1975, surrounded by bougainvillea in bright deep pink with its mild yet unforgettable honey scent.

As he puffed his cigarillo, Stefanos watched his young, strong, handsome, long-haired companion, who wore denim shorts and a sleeveless, pale blue shirt. *Yes, he could be my son,* he thought dreamily, *we have a deep connection; an extraordinary mutual understanding – even without words. He is my son – or, to put it correctly: he is my son, but in a different sense.*

"Roman, do you remember when you arrived in Mandraki you had a moment of strange and intense clarity? You saw something different in me than what I am now. Isn't that so?"

Roman took another sip of the tart and yet slightly sweet red wine from the blue-white glass with patterns that seemed more Turkish than Greek. He looked into Stefanos' eyes, whose colour and depth reflected the Aegean Sea.

"Yes, it was almost scary. It was as if I knew you from a very different, far away time."

"So it is, my son. What we perceive as time and space in this life is a helpful structure for our daily lives. However, the ancient sages taught us that this is only a tiny part of the reality of the universe – and thus of life itself. Life – and therefore our individual, real existence – takes place outside of time and space. That's why it's possible to remember something that we don't really know about in the here and now.

"And thus, you recognized me in another life, or another dimension, or another reality. I saw that too, Roman. You were – or are on another level – my son. It is an immeasurable joy for me to have you near me."

Roman took another sip of red wine. "It sounds crazy, somehow, because such thought processes are absolutely unusual for most of us. I don't know anyone who thinks or speaks like that. And yet, and yet... it's true! I know it from deep in my soul, not from the mind. And, Stefanos, I saw a star on your forehead – what was that about?"

"Atlantis, Roman. Atlantis!"

For a long moment they were both completely silent. Then Stefanos burst into his roaring laughter, and Roman couldn't help it, he also laughed in complete surrender. It was like a concert: the music of true friendship. Stefanos raised his glass:

"Roman, it's like this: all legends, myths, stories, fairy tales always point to something that may not be obvious. Oh, the great Greek legends with their pantheon of gods; the colourful legends of the Indians; the profound myths of the Inca and the Maya. Even Scandinavian mythology – think of the poetry and prose of the two Eddas!"

Stefano's eyes lit up, he took a deep breath, drank a sip of red wine. Roman was thrilled by this conversation, this different perspective, and added enthusiastically: "And what about JRR Tolkien? His brilliant, unique story of Middle Earth – including its cosmology, peoples and languages! A whole mythology!" And after a moment he added wistfully: "I wish the Elves were still here – and I was one of them..."

"My friend, we could talk about Tolkien's work for weeks to come, couldn't we? It is a world behind or above or before a world – full of poetry and brilliance and secrets of another reality... And there are so many other tales of different worlds: we can also add all the fairy tales, from the brothers Grimm and Hans Christian Andersen to Thousand and One Night and Le Petit Prince of Saint-Exupéry. And let's not forget Hermann Hesse, with his best-selling novel Siddharta – what a story, based on different levels, realities."

"And what do you think, Stefanos – also Christian mythology? The stories of Jesus are actually a myth, aren't they? Or Atlantis? I don't know the fairy tales from Asia and Africa, but I know that there are legends, sagas, myths everywhere. Yes, even in small Switzerland!"

"It is just so, Roman. There are legends and fairy tales all over the world. Fantastic stories, all pointing to something, trying to teach us something. As I once told Natalie: 'Look beyond the pictures you see. Think deeper than your thoughts. Listen beyond the words you hear. Remember what you have always known....' –

"There, my friend, lives life, lives the truth of the universe. Everything is happening at the same time, always there, interconnected, interwoven, possible, infinite... And so, it's no wonder that you and I have a story that goes much further than it seems." Stefanos needed a red wine break. Roman's gaze had drifted away. "Ah, I see, fíle mou, you also have other questions. Natalie..."

"Yes," said Roman, lost in thought. "My beloved mountain faery... it's been so long now... There were moments when I didn't know if it would make any sense to kidnap Natalie to Canada, so to speak. Denise and even Kurt had done everything they could to stop our relationship. Sometimes Natalie hadn't written for months. And I was so busy with Sean's ranch and somehow, I just lived there and in those moments..."

The Aegean Sea shone azure and indifferent this evening in the distance. Mysteriously as in a fairy tale, a gentle breeze carried the bright bells of the 15th century Agia Triada, the picturesque little church, to the two friends. Stefanos lit another cigarillo, poured more wine and probed:

"Fíle mou, can you imagine that there is much more to your story than you could be aware of? That in spite of the hurdles and detours and sabotage attempts – or perhaps because of them! – your paths had to come together in order to follow a common call?"

Stefanos came to an unexpected stop. The cigarillo almost fell out of his mouth. Although the evening sky over the Aegean was soft and clear, for a split second Natalie's uncle had seen lightning and thunder in a violent storm in a pitch black night. *There is something,* he thought, *something that makes the words I just said to Roman untruth. I don't know – but I'm sure the gods have*

shuffled the cards again... I cannot and don't want to tell
Roman.

Roman looked at Stefanos without understanding.
"What's going on, Stefanos? You seem far away."

"Yes, I'm sorry. Memories came up. You know, I, too,
had loved a wonderful young woman – so long ago, in
Berkeley, where I met Kurt, … Audrey..." Stefanos
sighed. "But that's a different story."

His ocean-blue eyes winked in his beautiful, wrinkled
face: "Let's talk about the story of Natalie and you. Despite all odds, you'll see your mountain faery again in a
few weeks. It's time, Roman."

Roman's laconic answer was only, "I know."

Until late into the Greek night punctuated with myriads
of brilliant stars, with red wine and ouzo, the two told
each other their stories and their dreams. Two friends,
who had found each other beyond time and space.

10

On the same evening in June 1975, three young women enjoyed a cold beer in the restaurant Gifthüttli in Basel: Natalie, Margo and Maja.

"Well", Maja began, "how does it feel to have a certain Swiss mountain lad from Canada almost on your doorstep after five years, Natalie?"

Natalie forced a smile, she felt insecure, overwhelmed, excited, joyful, gloomy and agitated. "To be honest, I'm completely confused. How many times in these five years – a long time, really... – have I thought about what it will be like when we meet again. Whether we'll meet again. And where. I've dreamed about it; I've imagined it; I've also wondered if it's even right. I'm sure we've both changed in the meantime. My Roman is still the one I met at the Silvretta. We had one single night of sweet lovemaking together. In Room #1...

Maja and Margo looked at each other: neither of them had ever seen Natalie in tears in public. Luckily, the lighting in the Gifthüttli was rather dim. Natalie was more than happy about it. As the other two wrapped themselves in meaningful silence, she began anew:

"All right, you two. The last few years have been quite the emotional roller-coaster ride. Nevertheless, with this deeper knowledge, or if you like, in my gut, I know that Roman and I belong together. You know what Mama and Papi think about it. But it doesn't matter. I also think Papi himself doesn't mind that we're still together and are now finally emigrating to Canada. Imagine this: In the Canadian North, in a log house Roman built himself, by the soft yellow light of candles and oil lamps and in the warmth of the roaring fire in the hearth – my great love and I!"

"How can it get any better than this!?" That was Maja.

Margo still had a knack of rolling her eyes impressively. "Yes, it sounds so romantic, doesn't it. Then add to that the freezing cold and the deep snow and the daily splitting of firewood... and in the summer the bears and the wolves and the mosquitoes." The three women burst into a liberating laugh.

"By the way: where is Roman at the moment?» Maja asked.

Natalie didn't know. "Somewhere on his way to Switzerland. His last letter was from Fort St. John, and that was several weeks ago. Maybe he went to visit Wally again... Anyway, he will arrive at Kloten Airport on July 18th – that's exactly one month from now! And then we'll go straight to Klosters. He has already booked a room at the Silvretta!"

"Let's toast to that!" Maja waved to Yvonne, the small, warm, brunette waitress, who immediately brought three more pints of Warteck beer. "To the Mystery called Life with all the adventures and surprises, joys and tears – and to love!" In the background the Bee Gees sang 'To Love Somebody'.

"Cheers!"

"So, switching subject." Margo suggested. "The world is changing: the Vietnam War is over! In England, for the first time, a woman has been elected as Leader of the Conservative Party – not that I think Margaret Thatcher is that great, but... And the rock group Queen has produced the most astonishing song: Bohemian Rhapsody. You have to hear it, girls, it is stunning!"

Maja: "Yes, imagine, after decades of atrocities and more than three million deaths, the Vietnam War is over. Saigon has fallen. The Americans are leaving. Long live Woodstock and the peace movement. May the Hippies rule the world! I haven't given up hope yet. And in that sense: have you two seen the musical Jesus Christ Superstar? Great! Hippie-like too; Roman would love it."

"Yes! And you know what, Maja?" Margo, who now wore her blonde hair in one beautifully braided plait, was on a roll. "Roman has a certain resemblance to the actor who portrays Jesus. Not only physically, but also as a human being. Natalie and I talked about it right after we saw the musical in the cinema. Super movie, yes. Throughout the Hippie movement, as well as in this film, the hope – or even the belief – for a better world, for peace and unity is repeated. It has to be possible!"

Maja: "May it be so!"

On the way home through the glinting lights of Basel by night, Natalie felt a peace within herself that she had long been missing. Maja and Margo were important pole stars in her life, even though she would seldom admit it to herself. The two had given her the confidence to embrace the unknown, this new life waiting for her. She recalled a sentence Stefanos had recently written in a letter: *The most decisive times in our lives are often those of great change. We have to approach them with courage and fearlessness.*

Natalie smiled. She saw the kind, sunburnt face of Stefanos in front of her and the glitter of his blue eyes. *Thank you, Uncle Stefanos, efcharistó!*

Having arrived safely at her home, Natalie slipped under her cuddly down blanket. In a month, Roman would be with her...

11

Roman thought for a long time about Stefanos' words: *We are the stories we tell each other about ourselves. It's like in a movie: we are the directors – and the actors. Is that reality? Are the dramas in our lives real? Behind the screen or backdrop of our lives is life. There is the source of all reality.*

Roman sat on a thick, night-blue pillow on the floor of his little room in Stefanos' cozy home and thought: *Not an easy concept.* He took out his notebook and wrote on his knees:

15 July 1975
I've been here on Nisyros for six weeks already. Up on the mountain in Nikia – overlooking the Stefanos crater of the volcano deep below me. The azure Aegean Sea all around. Oh, the many wonderful conversations with Stefanos! The walks on the dry, steep slopes of this island, where

again and again, and so unexpectedly, a delicate flower blooms white or pink in the shade of an olive tree. Swimming in the clear sea water, often alone with numerous small fish. How can I leave all this?

Like Stefanos said: stories. We make up our own stories... I'm sure he was trying to hint at something that is difficult or sheer impossible to express in words. But in this, there is a core of distant, unattainable truth that touches me deeply. With that in mind comes the next chapter in my story. Or better yet – I am writing the next chapter: Natalie, my mountain faery.

Is it really up to me to decide how my story goes? I think Stefanos' insights are both valuable and meaningful. However, he also sometimes speaks of the hand of the gods playing their cards. Is it on the stage of this world or behind the scenes? And if I take a step back and look into the far horizon of infinity – then the universe takes its course, no matter what...

This last thought, that the universe does what a universe does – no matter what we humans do or think – is a profound relief. The letting go of our false human arrogance is the opportunity to feel gratitude and even awe in the face of the immensity of the cosmos and of life in general. And live accordingly.

Stefanos may sometimes have the impression that I'm a slow learner. I actually feel like I am in a master's school and I'm barely making it through the class...

And now I should pack. With sadness, with parting sorrow, with gratitude – and with joy for the next chapter. May the gods and the universe guide me.

Stefanos had a jug of the tart red wine, which Roman loved by now, ready on the veranda table.

"Farewell is at hand, fíle mou. You have enriched my days, my son. It was and still is a great joy for me to have met you again. For me, at any rate, it is a reunion in the infinity of the mystery that we call life. Jámas!"

In this warm, blue Greek night, with wine and friend-ship, Roman remembered a poem.

Wind

The wind is my ally
my nature, my essence
I love the wind
as kin

What am I but the wind?

There is no-one there
when I let go
of the story line
just limitless flow
soaring freedom
cry of the eagle
storm on the horizon
changing shape and direction
on a whim

– Maja Rim

Part Three – Stone Circle

1

Natalie had no idea she could be so excited. It was July 18, 1975, a Friday, and this was it: today she would see Roman again!

She was standing in front of the round mirror in her bedroom in Basel, which assured her that her dark-blonde curls were as wild as ever and that her light denim summer dress was a perfect match. Her feelings were still confused. Even today, as so often in the past five years, she simply did not want to go any further. She wanted to continue her ordinary, pleasant life here and forget about Roman.

Natalie had tried this several times, especially at Mama's insistence. She hadn't written any letters to Roman for many long months. Her focus had been on school, the college education to become a geriatric nurse, her friends and her books. In addition to Hesse, she also began to read Tolkien, whom she greatly admired. Ah, now she could dive into new, strange worlds and forget everything else. She no longer travelled to Klosters, although her parents and Margo continued to spend their summer and winter holidays at the Silvretta.

Both Maja and Margo, and especially Stefanos, brought Natalie back to what was most important: her love for Roman and the possibility of living with him the way she imagined it could be. In harmony with nature, self-sufficient and as an example for others how to live a good life, how to shape it with a natural, common-sense approach. When the flame was rekindled, Natalie knew it was the only way she would have a fulfilling life. And if she was completely honest with herself, that would only be possible with Roman.

Some of Natalie's books and dishes, clothes and underwear were already packed in cardboard boxes. After their vacation in Klosters, Roman wanted to return to Canada as soon as possible. Of course, they would marry at the registry office of the municipality of Klosters.

After that, they would finally be able to apply for a permanent resident visa for Natalie.

With a packed backpack on her back, Natalie was already in the hallway when the phone rang. She had given herself enough time, so she could easily spare a few minutes. It was Maja.

"Listen girlfriend, I know you're nervous. Just briefly: '...and there's magic in every beginning...' Call me, sometime this week. Ciao. I love you."

"Thank you, Maja, for everything. Yes, I'll call you. Ciao, ciao cara."

* * *

Zurich-Kloten Airport. Wonderful, again and again, that atmosphere of flying. Travelling to other countries, other worlds, Natalie thought. The butterflies in her belly fluttered incessantly. It seemed completely unreal to her that Roman was about to come through the door. When she saw him, it was like an electric shock:

This tall, broad-shouldered, tanned man with his chestnut hair, interspersed with dazzling highlights of sunshine, which fell over the collar of his white cotton shirt... Yes, it was Roman. His mischievous, slightly crooked smile, the fine moustache and the small beard on his chin she used to call 'Jesus beard' – then she was in his arms. "My mountain faery..."

Natalie told Maja much later of this moment: "It was really like in the movies... As if shooting stars burst everywhere. It was like champagne bubbling up inside me. When Roman took my hand after the first long kiss, I knew without a doubt that our life would go on together. What a relief!"

Roman grabbed his oversized red backpack, and hand in hand, laughing and exuberant in their joy of being with each other, they took the tram to Zurich Central Station. There they stowed their backpacks, purchased their train tickets – SBB to Landquart, then the Rhaetian Railway to Klosters – and went to eat a peaceful lunch right at the train station.

Neither Natalie nor Roman could really believe that they were together now. No more separation.

"You know, Natalie, when I went through passport control, I had a moment of absolute panic. What if she's not there? – But you are here, my mountain faery! You are here..."

2

February 20, 2022

Sunday morning. The homely tolling of church bells and the cold winter mountain air floated through the open window. Natalie had dreamt of that day in July when she saw Roman for the first time after those long years. It had been one of those dreams that seemed so real that reality somehow shifted – or existed on different levels.

Natalie's memories of that July 18, 1975 were clear as a mountain stream. But for the moment she let them slide back into the treasury of her inner fortress like clouds of mist. With strong coffee and a croissant in the bed of the cozy and now familiar room overlooking the park, it was, thankfully, not that difficult. Today she just wanted to enjoy Klosters.

Directly opposite the Silvretta Parkhotel one could see the Älpeltispitz (about 2600 m), which was fairly easy to hike in summer and offered a magnificent view of the

Prättigauer and Davos mountains and valleys. Today it was brilliantly white like its neighbour, the Versitspitz. In the V-shaped valley between them, it was not unusual for several avalanches to thunder down after a heavy snow fall. For Natalie, the image of these two mountains had been the epitome of Klosters since her youth.

A little further to the North was the Madrisa with the striking peak of the Madrisahorn in the background. Austria was just beyond it, so to speak. A couple of years ago, in a letter to Natalie, Roman wrote down the legend of Madrisa, which his father had told him as a child:

In the old days, over in the Saas Alp at the foot of the Madrisahorn, a wealthy farmer had an alpine pasture. He sent his son up to stay there in the winter with the cows, as long as the supply of hay was sufficient, as is still the custom today.

A long time passed, but there was no news from the young man. The father feared that something bad might have befallen him, and set out in deep snow to look for him. He found his son busy with the dairy and was amazed at the abundant supply of milk, butter and cheese, and at the stately appearance of the cattle. "How is it," he asked, "that the cows are so smooth and beautiful and give milk as in summer?"

"That's what my Madrisa does," said the young man, "she searched for roots and herbs, which make the cattle so glossy and why they give so much milk." — "Who is this, your Madrisa?" The lad pointed to the half-open door of the chamber, and there lay sleeping on the bed a girl of marvellous beauty, whose fair hair fell all the way to the ground.

A cry of astonishment escaped the father. The girl awoke, got up, and walked toward them, saying, "If you had left me alone and in peace, it would have been better for you and your herd. It is with regret that I return from the warm hut to the woods and rocks, but I must."

She walked lightly over the snow towards the rocky peaks that looked like horns and disappeared. Today, they bear her name.

Roman had mentioned that the love between two people does not want to be disturbed by anyone uninitiated. Natalie thought this comment referred to her mother, who had been trying for years to bring her daughter to her senses. In spite of everything, Natalie had never lost her love for Mama.

It was high time to leave the wonderfully warm bed to live up to the radiant winter day. But Natalie didn't want to do too much today. Yesterday, she felt that her heart had been beating a bit too hard while snowshoeing on the Madrisa. So today, maybe just a walk along the Landquart to Aeuja and back. And then coffee and cake at the bakery Kaffeeklatsch.

But tomorrow morning, she would go snowshoeing to the Stone Circle and do what she had meant to do for a long time. She wanted to be back at the Silvretta early afternoon, as Maja was supposed to arrive in the evening.

"Hello my dear! On which train will you arrive in Klosters tomorrow?"

"Well, grüazi my friend! As far as I know, 15:58; so, four o'clock in the afternoon. Is that OK?"

"Yes, of course, Maja. I'll pick you up from the train station. In the morning I'm going to hike with my snow-shoes from Monbiel to the Stone Circle – I've already told you about it – and should be back at the hotel around 2 pm. Everything else tomorrow! Can't wait!"

"Me neither! Ciao bella, see you tomorrow!"

3

Friday, July 18, 1975

Natalie and Roman had quietly and companionably enjoyed their Cordon Bleu at the Brasserie Federal in Zurich Central Station, accompanied, of course, by a few
pints of beer: from the Bernese Müntschi to the Appen-
zell IPA. It was delicious just being together. After a lei-
surely stroll along the Uto Quai, watching the many
swans and revelling in sweet, tender moments in the
grass, Roman remarked without any sign of urgency:

"My dear mountain faery, I see thunderclouds coming
up. Let's go. Our train doesn't leave until half past eight,
but we can have another beer somewhere dry. And then
Klosters and the Silvretta! It has been so long..."

Arm in arm, the two strolled back to the station. As
usual, it was teeming with travellers, the forest green
SBB trains groaned and shrieked when they arrived, and
it smelled of iron and cigarette smoke and grilled

bratwurst. *Everything is so banal,* Natalie pondered while she couldn't stop looking at Roman's distinctive profile again and again, *and yet it is somehow magical. Everything's magical today.*

Natalie and Roman rode in first class. Even in the Rhaetian Railway. The seats were plush and comfortable, a kind of purple splendour. "It's time for me to spoil you, sweetheart," Roman said. Natalie still couldn't believe that she was now all cuddled up to Roman on the train to Klosters. They had long since left Lake Zurich and Lake Walensee behind, and now the RhB, having left Landquart, was winding its way up the Prättigau.

It was already dark outside, the lights of the small villages like Seewis, Grüsch and Schiers rushed past, but Roman did not see them. His thoughts and eyes were completely captured by Natalie. *Stefanos, thank you!* he thought, *without your advice and wisdom I might not be here. And I need to be here with Natalie – I understand this now deep down in my soul.*

"Did I ever tell you that I had been thinking about you all through those past five years, Natalie? Sure, I wanted to go to Canada, embark on an adventure, learn new and exciting things; how to live in the wilderness, the North. But I also wanted to prepare the way for us and our mission in this life.

"Speaking of which: Could you envision that there may be other realities besides this life here? I mean, time and space are relative anyway, so we could, so to speak, exist in other worlds or spheres at the same time – what do you think?" These thoughts, of course, partly reflected Stefanos' ideas, but Roman and Stefanos had sworn a sacred oath that neither of them would talk about their meeting each other to Natalie.

There they were again, the fancy thoughts of Roman. How Natalie still loved his unusual ways. "Hmm, I can't really imagine it, but so much is possible in this universe that seems inconceivable to our tiny human brain – why not? What are you referring to?"

"I wonder if I know you from somewhere else, from a different time or space, in a different way. It often appears to me that you are much more familiar to me than seems possible in our short time together. As if there was another life in which we knew each other, but it is obscured by a kind of veil... – wow, that was a loud bang of thunder!"

It was only then that Natalie and Roman noticed that the gods of thunder were bowling outside with joyful force, that it was raining in torrents and that lightning ripped the darkness apart. "A stormy night!" said Roman, "Great! It's fitting for our reunion, isn't it, my mountain faery." Roman held Natalie's hands and looked into her green eyes, "I love you, Natalie. And nothing and no one will ever change that!"

A blissful, inner exuberance spread throughout Natalie's body. The questioning and the tears of the past five years poured like rain into the foaming Landquart outside. This was why she had persevered. They were together again, they were going to return to Klosters, to the Hotel Silvretta, where it all began. And they were going to get married. After a long, languid kiss, Roman got up to go to the bathroom.

Natalie looked out the window, rain streaming down the glass, but all she saw was her own face, radiant, happy, smiling.

And then – NOTHING.

4

Natalie did not know how she came to. Whether it had been seconds or hours. Even later, she could not explain in words how it had felt. It had not really been a darkness she had fallen into. It was complete nothingness. All memory erased. She only knew that something must have happened: the train had stopped running. It appeared to move forward, though, in abrupt, startling intervals and it seemed to be lopsided.

Her head hurt and apparently she had a nosebleed. The light in their wagon flickered, went off at times and then on again. Outside, the thunderstorm was still raging, rain was pelting on the windows and the eerie brightness of lightning strikes made everything resemble a bizarre science fiction show.

As if in a vaporous daze, Natalie kept watching the rain whip against the train windows that were illuminated almost without interruption by glittering lightning. The thunder crashed constantly and mercilessly like the volleys of an army. Natalie covered her ears with her hands. Only then did she realize she was sitting on the floor. Around her was a chaotic mess of suitcases, handbags and backpacks.

Panic gripped her. Roman! Where was Roman?

He had gone to the bathroom, Natalie remembered. Where was the bathroom? She had watched him leave their wagon toward the front of the train, so it must be in that direction. Another jolt shook the railcar and the few frightened people around her as she tried to get to her feet. Someone helped her up; she didn't see the person. Her mind was on one single track: find Roman.

Roman lay covered in blood in an aisle between the seats. An elderly man with a beret on his round, bald head knelt beside him. "Monsieur, monsieur, 'ow can I 'elp you, monsieur? Parlez-vous français, monsieur? Est-ce-que vous m'entendez?" Natalie arrived just when Roman made a slight nod with his head. She sank beside her future husband. "Roman! Roman! Do you recognize me?"

The light flickered – and went out. Natalie could only see by the lightning strikes that continued unperturbed to rip the night apart. Followed by thunder crashing with a force that was physically palpable. She kept on stroking Roman's blood-soaked hair, while the train rocked sideways and forward. Someone screamed: "Get out! We all have to get out! Now!"

Flailing in the flickering flashes of the lightning bolts, Natalie, the gentleman with the beret and a younger man with thick arms like a woodcutter picked Roman up as gently as they could. Another passenger had managed to open the door despite the hysteric confusion, and together they managed to carry Roman outside into the deluge. They laid him on a coat, that one of the angels of this train had placed on the soaking grass. The man who looked like a lumberjack took off his leather jacket and covered Roman.

Natalie was kneeling beside him, rain and tears pouring down her face. Roman's hazel eyes were open, but he could not speak. He tried a little smile, though, which gave Natalie everything she needed at the moment. She barely noticed how several people ran back and forth in dismay, how the wagons of Express Train 91 rocked in jolts and slowly slid more and more towards the Landquart. The thunderstorm continued to rage, and the rain kept pouring on the passengers, who were all desperately waiting for help. Some of them had dared to return to the train to haul out all the luggage they found. One of those pieces was Roman's big red backpack.

It had been completely surreal, even in Natalie's memory.

5

Natalie never wrote journals or notebooks like Roman had all his life. But in the days following the train crash, writing was the only way for her to express her inner turmoil:

July 20, 1975

Two days ago, I saw Roman again after five long and sometimes lonely years. Oh, how exuberant we were! How insanely happy to be together, to return to Klosters, where we had fallen in love six years ago. And then, after our wedding, we would fly to Canada and begin to live our dream in the Yukon Territory.

Facts:

Today in 'Die Tat' there is a short article with a photo of the railway accident. It looks awful.

As the Rhätische Bahn announced after the accident, a mountain stream swollen by the severe thunderstorm had washed away part of the railway tracks between Fideris and Küblis that night. Our train, the last one of the day, thus rattled off the rails – into the torrential waters of the Landquart.

The locomotive immediately plunged into the floods of the Landquart, the wagons slowly followed and hung lopsided on the slope. Fortunately, the doors could be opened manually. The 16 passengers and the conductor were able to escape. The driver was found dead in the locomotive, which was under water.

The accident site was near the country road leading to Klosters and Davos. As I recall, all passing cars stopped. I didn't want to wait for the police or the ambulance and accepted the offer of a local man to drive Roman and me to Klosters. I don't know his name. I don't remember his face at all. Only his calm Prättigauer voice, which gave me comfort.

I had put Roman's head on my lap, he breathed calmly with his eyes closed. When he opened them just before we arrived at the Silvretta in Klosters, it was as if he was passing all his love and his whole being on to me. Then his beautiful eyes broke, and I knew he had left this world.

I don't know how to handle it. Roman is dead. I have to write it this way. He's gone from here. Our home in Canada will never be our home now. Our plans for permaculture, a simple life in and with nature – everything has been swallowed by this insane moment none of us are ever prepared for.

It can't be. It just can't be true. I see him coming into the room here at the Silvretta any minute. The door opens and it must be him. I see his half-smile, his left hand smoothing back a strand of his long hair. I feel his strong arms holding me close. And I hear his sonorous voice with the Bündner dialect telling me it was all just a horrible night-mare. That everything is alright now.

But it isn't. Roman is dead. I will never see him in this life again. Only in my dreams... Maja is here; the gods be great thanks for that. And yet, I feel as if there is no solid ground beneath my feet. I have no perspective. There is a stabbing pain inside me, but I'm numb, exhausted, cold.

Maja arrived already yesterday. Papi took her along in the car. They are both here at the hotel. I am not alone. But I am. I want to scream, but I am too exhausted. They told me that Roman's body is in a cold room at Schiers Hospital. And that he will be cremated in Chur in a few days. I can't think about it. I don't want to think about it. It just cannot be!

If only Stefanos were here. I need to talk to him somehow. He would be the only person who could possibly make sense of or find an explanation for this totally absurd craziness.

They brought me Roman's backpack; his notebooks are all in there. I can't look at them.

I'm going down to the bar now with Maja and Papi for a glass of Whisky. Or two.

6

On July 30, 12 days after the train accident, Roman's Celebration of Life was held in Sent. Natalie and Anna, Roman's mother, met for the first time. "I would have loved to have known you in Roman's lifetime, dear..." Anna sobbed, but she managed a small smile. On a steep hill above the village, the two unequal women, hand in hand, released some of Roman's ashes in the wind.

Then Anna held out with both hands a small, artful, hand-carved wooden chest to Natalie. "This is for you, Natalie. So that you also have a part of his ashes." There was so much sadness and kindness in the eyes of the little, stout woman, and the look reminded Natalie so much of Roman that she had trouble swallowing the lump in her throat. The two women, who had never seen each other before, embraced like lifelong friends.

Maja and Margo, Papi and Mama, Dumeng of course, Roman's closest friend, even Gino, Roman's former waiter-colleague, the Roccos from Hotel Silvretta in Klosters and many friends and relatives of the Camenischs, whom Natalie did not know, stood silently in the grass. Sun, wind and tears accompanied Roman's ashes into the breath of the universe. And as if from far away, yet close, the song 'Gethsemane' from the musical Jesus Christ Superstar sounded softly. Roman had once written to Natalie that he was deeply touched by this music. And Maja knew that.

Natalie, her family and Maja did not return to Klosters until the next day. The magnificent vistas on the ride over the Flüela Pass were like an unreal scenery for Natalie, a beautiful backdrop. She leaned against Maja and closed her eyes. She held on to the lovely wooden box with Roman's precious ashes. It was not him, she knew that, of course. But it was something of him she could hold. *I don't know how I am going to get through this,* she thought in a haze of sorrow and lingering disbelief. *I just don't know how, Roman. I don't know how.*

When Natalie opened her eyes again, Papi had already parked his latest Chrysler just outside the Silvretta in Klosters. In front of the hotel stood a man in a white cotton shirt, enhancing his bronze face and azure eyes. Natalie would never know who had notified Stefanos. Or when, or if, or how. She stumbled out of the car and fell into his arms. Finally, finally she could let go and allow the flood of her tears to flow.

"Agapiméni mou!"

7

2022

The break of day was so quiet and calm. In the light of the waning moon the mountains glittered like mother of pearl. It was Monday, February 21, 2022, and Natalie was in bed in her room facing the park at the Silvretta Parkhotel. She had not slept well. Today she wanted to bring Roman's ashes and the braided leather bracelet he had given her in August 1969 to the Stone Circle. The memory of the train accident and Roman's sudden death was so clear again that tears burned behind her eyelids.

She was sure that she would not have found her way back to life without Stefanos' help. His surprise arrival at Klosters had been like a solid rope over the bottomless chasm from which he had pulled her up. Or maybe even a suspension bridge over which she was able to cross this merciless abyss.

Five days later, I was already on my way to Nisyros with Stefanos, Natalie remembered, *it was the absolutely right thing to do. And even though I had no idea at the time that Roman had been with Stefanos only recently for several weeks, I felt the closeness of my love immediately. And now I understand why. Roman was there, with me, around me, within me. It was a bit unnerving at times, but I just surrendered to that warm, familiar feeling of him.*

Stefanos, you beloved, wise man! You made me cry and sob and moan. You always held me with your open heart, which – as I know now! – was also broken, and comforted me. You spoke to me for hours and you let me talk for hours. In the first few days, I hid in my pretty, whitewashed room in the evenings, under the turquoise, hand-woven cotton blanket. You left me alone there until the sun went down. And then you gathered me in with your strong, soft arms, you took me outside to the veranda and fed me with souvlaki and red wine. I remember it well.

You told me energy could never be lost in this universe. And that we are ultimately all pure energy. Therefore, Roman's energetic being is still here, somewhere, somehow. And I know that's true. His role in this reality was fulfilled, you mentioned. Even though his and my future in Canada did not come about. Love is love. That power will always be there. It doesn't matter if the person exists here in this reality. What matters is that we __are__ love, unselfish, benevolent and responsible. You had explained this to me a long, long time ago.

Efcharistó, Stefanos! I owe you my life and my understanding of life. And now that I know Roman was with you, the circle is complete.

* * *

Natalie got up and ordered her breakfast. A strong coffee would do her good. She had stayed with Stefanos for six months. In her memory it had been just a few days, mostly in azure blue, adorned with pink bougainvillea and in the security of Stefanos' love. She would never forget his bouncing, silver-grey moustache in his dark, wrinkled

face and his resounding laugh. She had returned to Nisyros many times since and before he, too, died many
years ago. Natalie carried Roman's and Stefanos' love
within her as precious reminders of the mysteries. And as
an inner refuge that she could return to anytime she
needed to. How fortunate she felt. How privileged.

The small, friendly, blond waiter brought her coffee
with Gipfeli, and she gave him a smile. Strengthened,
dressed warmly, equipped with a backpack and snowshoes, Natalie set out for the Postauto stop at a quarter
to nine o'clock.

8

It was cold in Monbiel because the sun was not high enough to reach the valley this early. It's cold inside me too, Natalie thought, as if I were about to say goodbye. She hardly noticed that the trees were wearing a magnificent, sparkling dress of ice crystals.

Natalie had crossed the young Landquart via the Pardenner Brüggli and was now on her way to the meadow where Roman had kissed her for the first time. Her sobbing frightened two deer, who rushed away through the high snow. "Sorry, my friends," she said instinctively.

There it was, Juan Rios' Stone Circle of Water. Back then, in 1969, it didn't exist yet. Natalie knew that diagonally opposite on the right side of the river, on the Pardenner Hexenbödeli, was the Circle of Fire. Juan Rios once said, *'...the Stone Circle is an attempt to build a bridge between us and our other reality.'*

Yes, Natalie thought, I'm actually trying to do exactly that today. She had brought a woollen blanket, which she spread on the snow in front of one of the eight stones. Some of the subtle paintings on the stones were still visible: spirals, circles, triangles. Natalie felt like she had stepped into another world. As if this reality were only one of many. Stefanos had repeatedly hinted that there were other dimensions behind the façade of this world. Even Roman had spoken of 'other spheres' on that fatal train ride in July 1975.

Sitting on the wool blanket, Natalie unpacked the leather bracelet and the exquisite wooden box with Roman's ashes. She held both in her hands for a while, imbued with feelings ranging from deep sadness to astonishment to boundless gratitude.

"Thank you Roman," she said softly, "for your love. You were, are and always will be a part of me. And thank you Stefanos, for your accompanying and guiding both of us in kindness and wisdom."

Natalie got up, left her backpack on the blanket, and walked on snowshoes to the bank of the Landquart. She opened the box and with a single swing she left Roman's ashes to the light winter breeze. Roman's remains floated away as if weightless, some of them settling lightly on the snow or drifting ephemerally on the surface of the Landquart.

It was done.

The leather bracelet with the glass beads was still in her left hand when she sat down again on the woollen blanket and leaned against the large stone in the circle of the others. She drank a sip of hot herbal tea, which she had brought with her in the thermos. Very softly she seemed to hear Stefanos' beloved voice: "Agapiméni mou."

Her heartbeat was fast, as if she had exerted herself. Only briefly she felt a stabbing pain and automatically clutched her heart with her right hand. Then the spruce trees and Juan Rios' stones seemed to fade as if in a bright, glimmering mist. The bubbly noise of the Land-quart grew silent.

Little by little, she thought she saw a figure emerging from the mist. He was tall. The long, chestnut-brown hair fell on his broad shoulders, and a half-crooked smile played around his pretty mouth. Roman.

Natalie couldn't see him clearly; everything was so bright around them both. She got up and took his out-stretched hand into hers. She was young again and was wearing the lovely, flowery summer dress of that time long ago. In her left hand she held his leather bracelet. Roman took her in his arms.

The light became brighter.

And brighter.

And brighter.

9

Maja, her now white hair gathered in a knot, arrived at Klosters Platz on 21 February 2022 at 15:58 as planned. She loved the feeling of arriving in a different place. *Yes,* she thought, *Klosters is really fabulous, like a village from a fairy tale.* There were some people in ski suits at the station, but she couldn't see Natalie. When her friend was still not there at a quarter past four, she pulled out her cell phone. No answer.

Arriving at the Silvretta Parkhotel, she asked for Natalie at the reception. Anja, the friendly, black-haired young lady only knew that Natalie had left quite early in the morning. At Maja's suggestion, she called Christian Erpenbeck, the director and owner. He greeted Maja with a friendly smile from his grey eyes.

"Let's go up to the room and have a look, Mrs. Rim." With his long legs he was up the stairs in an instant, Maja followed almost as quickly. Christian Erpenbeck opened the door of # 408, the room to the park, as he called it, with his passepartout. Maja saw Natalie's things, a lot of notebooks that must have been Roman's – but Natalie was not there.

"She wanted to go to the Stone Circle behind Monbiel – maybe something happened to her." Maja was already thinking about planning a search operation.

"We're going to Monbiel in my car right away," the hotel director said. "Don't worry, we'll find her."

It was getting dark. With Christian Erpenbeck's four-wheel drive vehicle they were in Monbiel in a quarter of an hour, from where he continued to the junction to Garfiun. He had organized snowshoes, headlamps and two local friends. Over the Pardenner Brüggli – and they clearly saw Natalie's snowshoe trail. It led to the Stone Circle, and not back.

Maja wanted to go first, and the others let her. She saw Natalie at once, leaning against one of the big stones, her head had slid down to her left side. Maja had no thoughts – she knew in her heart that Natalie was dead. Kneeling in the snow next to her friend, she saw the backpack, the thermos and the open, empty wooden box.

"My beloved friend", she said softly to the silent person on the wool blanket, "you did it. You let him go – and through letting him go, you found him."

Epilogue

Three months later, Maja was sitting in the same Stone Circle with Natalie's ashes and Roman's notebooks. The leather bracelet, of which Natalie had often spoken, remained missing.

After silent moments of reflection, of uncounted precious memories surfacing, Maja stood up. "Though I am here in the Water Circle, I give these diaries to the fire," she said aloud to the stones.

Roman's notebooks burned and blazed, one by one. It was a mild May evening, the willows on the banks of the Landquart already had young, soft green leaves. Maja mixed the ashes of the notebooks with those of Natalie's in the clay jar, and let the wind carry them over the water and the meadows.

Then Maja said aloud the last words Stefanos had written to Natalie before his death:

... Remember, agapiméni mou, that everything in life, especially death, tragedy and injustice, have the appearance of reality. But they are not reality. They are stories we tell each other. Real life is behind the scenes, where there is no time or space. And that is where you are always united with Roman...

To close the circle she recited one of her own poems in her soft, melodious voice:

At the end

At the end of my days
I want to say
that I have lived it all

That I was maiden and mother and crone

That I was rosebush
and pine tree
and the lily in the field

That I was wild strawberry
on a child's tongue
nectar of lilac
luring the honey bee
and the lover in your
dreams

Ah, and that I was the honey bee, too
and the wolf, stalking the caribou
and the caribou, being hunted

That I have tasted joy
and despair
and everything in between

When the end is here
I want to say
that I have lived it all

And the mist rolls in from the river
enfolding me in
sweet silence

My Heartfelt Thanks!

Without YOU this book would not have been written and published:

Cynthia Chamberlin - Long-time Friend, language aficionada and eager editor of the English Edition.

Keith Beech - Long-time Friend, reluctant and gracious editor of the English Edition.

Esther & Reto Hubli - Friends and willing editors of the German Edition and first version of the story.

Doris Kara - My sister, who went through the German Edition with a fine-tooth comb in order to correct all those silly mistakes that find their way into a manuscript.

Urs Heinz Aerni - Switzerland's magician of anything written, who guided my way.

Christian Erpenbeck - Director and owner of the Silvretta Parkhotel, who showed me around the whole hotel and told me stories about the development from the old Hotel Silvretta to now – and who coined the title of the German Edition: *Das Zimmer zum Park*.

Dr. Jürg Stahel - Friend and guide to the old myths of this area and to Juan Rios' stone circles.

Dr. Christoph Luzi - Project Manager 800 Jahre Klosters, who kindly provided me with various sources of crucial information about the history of Klosters.

Yvonne Dünser - Media spokeswoman of the Rhätische Bahn, who kindly shared ample photos and information about the train accident in 1975.

The Rocco Family - The daughters of former owner and director of Hotel Silvretta, Giorgio Rocco, graciously allowed me to use his name in this story.

And, of course, so much gratitude to Maja and Stefanos... – Efcharistó!

* * *

*Stufen – Stages (page 104), translated into English by the author.
The poem *Stufen* by Hermann Hesse was reproduced by kind permission of Suhrkamp Verlag Berlin.
The original poem in German follows here:

Stufen

Wie jede Blüte welkt und jede Jugend
Dem Alter weicht, blüht jede Lebensstufe,
Blüht jede Weisheit auch und jede Tugend
Zu ihrer Zeit und darf nicht ewig dauern.
Es muß das Herz bei jedem Lebensrufe
Bereit zum Abschied sein und Neubeginne,
Um sich in Tapferkeit und ohne Trauern
In andre, neue Bindungen zu geben.
Und jedem Anfang wohnt ein Zauber inne,
Der uns beschützt und der uns hilft, zu leben.

Wir sollen heiter Raum um Raum durchschreiten,
An keinem wie an einer Heimat hängen,
Der Weltgeist will nicht fesseln uns und engen,
Er will uns Stuf' um Stufe heben, weiten.
Kaum sind wir heimisch einem Lebenskreise
Und traulich eingewohnt, so droht Erschlaffen,
Nur wer bereit zu Aufbruch ist und Reise,
Mag lähmender Gewöhnung sich entraffen.

Es wird vielleicht auch noch die Todesstunde
Uns neuen Räumen jung entgegen senden,
Des Lebens Ruf an uns wird niemals enden...
Wohlan denn, Herz, nimm Abschied und gesunde!

Evelyn Kaltenbach, born 1954 in Basel, Switzerland, immigrated to Canada 27 years later. Her work took her to several hotels and lodges, a schoolboard, a nurses' association and a wildlife preserve.

As a young teenager and avid reader, she began writing poems, journals and short stories. This is her second novel.

She has a daughter, two sons and two grandsons who all live in Canada.

Today, she makes her home in Klosters, Switzerland, and on the West Coast of Canada.

www.ingramcontent.com/pod-product-compliance
Lightning Source LLC
Chambersburg PA
CBHW051247250626

47155CB00009B/3201